Leveled Texts
for
Classic Fiction

Shakespeare

Rewritten by Tamara Hollingsworth

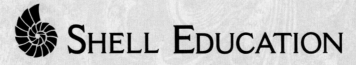
SHELL EDUCATION

Contributing Author

Wendy Conklin, M.S.

Publishing Credits

Dona Herweck Rice, *Editor-in-Chief*; Robin Erickson, *Production Director*;
Lee Aucoin, *Creative Director*; Timothy J. Bradley, *Illustration Manager*;
Sara Johnson, M.S.Ed., *Senior Editor*; Evelyn Garcia, *Associate Education Editor*;
Grace Alba, *Interior Layout Designer*; Stephanie Reid, *Photo Editor*;
Corinne Burton, M.A.Ed., *Publisher*

Image Credits

Cover The Bridgeman Art Library, Shutterstock; p. 31-38, 40, 42, 44, 46–54, 71–79, 81, 83, 85, 87–110, 120, 122, 124, 126, 127, 129, 131, 133, 135, 137, 139, 141, 144, 146, 148, 150 The Bridgeman Art Library; p. 56, 58, 60, 62 iStockphoto; p. 63, 65, 67, 69 Getty Images; p. 112 LOC [LC-USZC4-5221], 114 LOC [LC-USZC4-5221], 116 LOC [LC-USZC4-5221], 118 LOC [LC-USZC4-5221]; p. 128, 130, 132, 134, Mary Evans Picture Library/Alamy;
all other images Shutterstock

Standards

© 2004 Mid-continent Research for Education and Learning (McREL)
© 2010 National Governors Association Center for Best Practices and Council of Chief State School Officers (CCSS)

Shell Education

5301 Oceanus Drive
Huntington Beach, CA 92649

http://www.shelleducation.com

ISBN 978-1-4258-0982-9

© 2013 Shell Educational Publishing, Inc.

Table of Contents

#50982—*Leveled Texts for Classic Fiction: Shakespeare* © *Shell Education*

What Is Fiction?

Fiction is the work of imaginative narration. In other words, it is something that is made, as opposed to something that has happened or something that is discovered. It helps bring our imaginations to life, since it offers an escape into a world where everything happens for a reason—nothing is by chance. Fiction includes three main elements: plot (sequence), character, and setting (place).

Each event occurs in a logical order, and somehow, the conflict is resolved. Fiction promises a resolution in the end, and so the reader waits for resolution as the characters change, grow, and survive experiences. We are drawn to fiction because it is very close to the story of our lives. Fiction suggests that our own stories will have meaning and a resolution in the end. Perhaps that might be the reason why we love fiction—it delivers what it promises.

Fiction compels its readers to care about the characters whether they are loyal friends or conniving enemies. Readers dream about the characters and mourn their heartaches. Readers might feel that they know a fictional character's story intimately because he or she reminds them of a friend or family member. Additionally, the place described in the story might feel like a real place the reader has visited or would like to visit.

Fiction vs. Nonfiction

Fiction is literature that stems from the imagination and includes genres such as mystery, adventure, fairy tales, and fantasy. Fiction can include facts, but the story is not true in its entirety. Facts are often exaggerated or manipulated to suit an author's intent for the story. Realistic fiction uses plausible characters and storylines, but the people do not really exist and/ or the events narrated did not ever really take place. In addition, fiction is descriptive, elaborate, and designed to entertain. It allows readers to make their own interpretations based on the text.

Nonfiction includes a wide variety of writing styles that deal exclusively with real events, people, places, and things such as biographies, cookbooks, historical records, and scientific reports. Nonfiction is literature based on facts or perceived facts. In literature form, nonfiction deals with events that have actually taken place and relies on existing facts. Nonfiction writing is entirely fact-based. It states only enough to establish a fact or idea and is meant to be informative. Nonfiction is typically direct, clear, and simple in its message. Despite the differences, both fiction and nonfiction have a benefit and purpose for all readers.

The Importance of Using Fiction

Reading fiction has many benefits: It stimulates the imagination, promotes creative thinking, increases vocabulary, and improves writing skills. However, "students often hold negative attitudes about reading because of dull textbooks or being forced to read" (Bean 2000).

Fiction books can stimulate imagination. It is easy to get carried away with the character Percy Jackson as he battles the gods in *The Lightning Thief* (Riordan 2005). Readers can visualize what the author depicts. Researcher Keith Oatley (2009) states that fiction allows individuals to stimulate the minds of others in a sense of expanding on how characters might be feeling and what they might be thinking. When one reads fiction, one cannot help but visualize the nonexistent characters and places of the story. Lisa Zunshine (2006) has emphasized that fiction allows readers to engage in a theory-of-mind ability that helps them practice what the characters experience.

Since the work of fiction is indirect, it requires analysis if one is to get beyond the surface of the story. On the surface, one can view *Moby Dick* (Melville 1851) as an adventure story about a man hunting a whale. On closer examination and interpretation, the novel might be seen as a portrayal of good and evil. When a reader examines, interprets, and analyzes a work of fiction, he or she is promoting creative thinking. Creativity is a priceless commodity, as it facilitates problem solving, inventions, and creations of all kinds, and promotes personal satisfaction as well.

Reading fiction also helps readers build their vocabularies. Readers cannot help but learn a myriad of new words in Lemony Snicket's *A Series of Unfortunate Events* (1999). Word knowledge and reading comprehension go hand in hand. In fact, "vocabulary knowledge is one of the best predictors of reading achievement" (Richek 2005). Further, "vocabulary knowledge promotes reading fluency, boosts reading comprehension, improves academic achievement, and enhances thinking and communication" (Bromley 2004). Most researchers believe that students have the ability to add between 2,000 to 3,000 new words each school year, and by fifth grade, that number can be as high as 10,000 new words in their reading alone (Nagy and Anderson 1984). By exposing students to a variety of reading selections, educators can encourage students to promote the vocabulary growth that they need to be successful.

Finally, reading fictional text has a strong impact on students' ability as writers. According to Gay Su Pinnell (1988), "As children read and write, they make the connections that form their basic understandings about both….There is ample evidence to suggest that the processes are inseparable and that teachers should examine pedagogy in the light of these interrelationships." Many of the elements students encounter while reading fiction can transition into their writing abilities.

The Importance of Using Fiction *(cont.)*

Text Complexity

Text complexity refers to reading and comprehending various texts with increasing complexity as students progress through school and within their reading development. The Common Core State Standards (2010) state that "by the time they [students] complete the core, students must be able to read and comprehend independently and proficiently the kinds of complex texts commonly found in college and careers." In other words, by the time students complete high school, they must be able to read and comprehend highly complex texts, so students must consistently increase the level of complexity tackled at each grade level. Text complexity relies on the following combination of quantitative and qualitative factors:

Quantitative Factors	
Word Frequency	This is how often a particular word appears in the text. If an unfamiliar high-frequency word appears in a text, chances are the student will have a difficult time understanding the meaning of the text.
Sentence Length	Long sentences and sentences with embedded clauses require a lot from a young reader.
Word Length	This is the number of syllables in a word. Longer words are not by definition hard to read, but certainly can be for young readers.
Text Length	This refers to the number of words within the text passage.
Text Cohesion	This is the overall structure of the text. A high-cohesion text guides readers by signaling relationships among sentences through repetition and concrete language. A low-cohesion text does not have such support.

The Importance of Using Fiction (cont.)

Qualitative Factors	
Level of Meaning or Purpose of Text	This refers to the objective and/or purpose for reading.
Structure	Texts that display low complexity are known for their simple structure. Texts that display high complexity are known for disruptions to predictable understandings.
Language Convention and Clarity	Texts that deviate from contemporary use of English tend to be more challenging to interpret.
Knowledge Demands	This refers to the background knowledge students are expected to have prior to reading a text. Texts that require students to possess a certain amount of previous knowledge are more complex than those that assume students have no prior knowledge.

(Adapted from the National Governors Association Center for Best Practices and Council of Chief State School Officers 2010)

The use of qualitative and quantitative measures to assess text complexity is demonstrated in the expectation that educators possess the ability to match the appropriate texts to the appropriate students. The passages in *Leveled Texts for Classic Fiction: Shakespeare* vary in text complexity and will provide leveled versions of classic complex texts so that educators can scaffold students' comprehension of these texts. Educators can choose passages for students to read based on the reading level as well as the qualitative and quantitative complexity factors in order to find texts that are "just right" instructionally.

Genres of Fiction

There are many different fiction genres. The *Leveled Texts for Classic Fiction* series focuses on the following genres: adventure, fantasy and science fiction, mystery, historical fiction, mythology, humor, and Shakespeare.

Adventure stories transport readers to exotic places like deserted islands, treacherous mountains, and the high seas. This genre is dominated by fast-paced action. The plot often focuses on a hero's quest and features a posse that helps him or her achieve the goal. The story confronts the protagonist with events that disrupt his or her normal life and puts the character in danger. The story involves exploring and conquering the unknown accompanied by much physical action, excitement, and risk. The experience changes the protagonist in many ways.

 #50982—*Leveled Texts for Classic Fiction: Shakespeare*

The Importance of Using Fiction *(cont.)*

Fantasy and science fiction are closely related. Fantasy, like adventure, involves quests or journeys that the hero must undertake. Within fantasy, magic and the supernatural are central and are used to suggest universal truths. Events happen outside the laws that govern our universe. Science fiction also operates outside of the laws of physics but typically takes place in the future, space, another world, or an alternate dimension. Technology plays a strong role in this genre. Both science fiction and fantasy open up possibilities (such as living in outer space and talking to animals) because the boundaries of the real world cannot confine the story. Ideas are often expressed using symbols.

Mystery contains intriguing characters with suspenseful plots and can often feel very realistic. The story revolves around a problem or puzzle to solve: *Who did it? What is it? How did it happen?* Something is unknown, or a crime needs to be solved. Authors give readers clues to the solution in a mystery, but they also distract the reader by intentionally misleading them.

Historical fiction focuses on a time period from the past with the intent of offering insight into what it was like to live during that time. This genre incorporates historical research into the stories to make them feel believable. However, much of the story is fictionalized, whether it is conversations or characters. Often, these stories reveal that concerns from the past are still concerns. Historical fiction centers on historical events, periods, or figures.

Myths are collections of sacred stories from ancient societies. Myths are ways to explain questions about the creation of the world, the gods, and human life. For example, mythological stories often explain why natural events like storms or floods occur or how the world and living things came to be in existence. Myths can be filled with adventures conflict, between humans, and gods with extraordinary powers. These gods possess emotions and personality traits that are similar to humans.

Humor can include parody, joke books, spoofs, and twisted tales, among others. Humorous stories are written with the intent of being light-hearted and fun in order to make people laugh and to entertain. Often, these stories are written with satire and dry wit. Humorous stories also can have a very serious or dark side, but the ways in which the characters react and handle the situations make them humorous.

Shakespeare's plays can be classified in three genres: comedy, tragedy, and history. Shakespeare wrote his plays during the late 1500s and early 1600s, and performed many of them in the famous Globe Theater in London, England. Within each play is not just one coherent story but also a set of two or three stories that can be described as "plays within a play." His plays offer multiple perspectives and contradictions to make the stories rich and interesting. Shakespeare is noted for his ability to bring thoughts to life. He used his imagination to adapt stories, history, and other plays to entertain his audiences.

Elements of Fiction

The many common characteristics found throughout fiction are known as the elements of fiction. Among such elements are *point of view, character, setting,* and *plot. Leveled Texts for Classic Fiction* concentrates on setting, plot, and character, with an emphasis on language usage.

Language usage typically refers to the rules for making language. This series includes the following elements: *personification, hyperbole, alliteration, onomatopoeia, imagery, symbolism, metaphor,* and *word choice.* The table below provides a brief description of each.

Language Usage	Definition	Example
Personification	Giving human traits to nonhuman things	The chair moaned when she sat down on it.
Hyperbole	Extreme exaggeration	He was so hungry, he could eat a horse.
Alliteration	Repetition of the beginning consonant sounds	She sold seashells by the seashore.
Onomatopoeia	Forming a word from the sound it makes	Knock-knock, woof, bang, sizzle, hiss
Imagery	Language that creates a meaningful visual experience for the reader	His socks filled the room with a smell similar to a wet dog on a hot day.
Symbolism	Using objects to represent something else	A heart represents *love*.
Metaphor	Comparison of two unrelated things	My father is the rock of our family.
Word Choice	Words that an author uses to make the story memorable and to capture the reader's attention	In chapter two of *Holes* by Louis Sachar (2000), the author directly addresses the reader, saying, "The reader is probably asking…." The author predicts what the reader is wondering.

Elements of Fiction (cont.)

Setting is the *where* and *when* of a story's action. Understanding setting is important to the interpretation of the story. The setting takes readers to other times and places. Setting plays a large part in what makes a story enjoyable for the reader.

Plot forms the core of what the story is about and establishes the chain of events that unfolds in the story. Plot contains a character's motivation and the subsequent cause and effect of the character's actions. A plot diagram is an organizational tool that focuses on mapping out the events in a story. By mapping out the plot structure, students are able to visualize the key features of a story. The following is an example of a plot diagram:

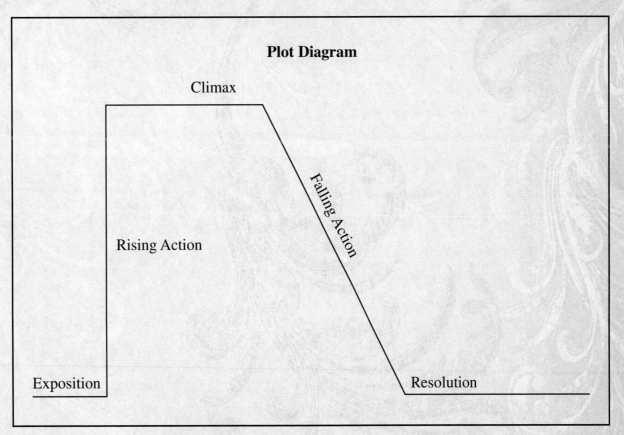

Plot Diagram

Climax

Rising Action

Falling Action

Exposition

Resolution

Characters are the people in the story. The protagonist is the main or leading character. He or she might be the narrator of the story. The antagonist is the force or character that acts against the protagonist. This antagonist is not always a person; it could be things such as weather, technology, or even a vehicle. Both the protagonist and antagonist can be considered dynamic, which means that they change or grow during the story as opposed to remaining static, or unchanging, characters. Readers engage with the text as they try to understand what motivates the characters to think and act as they do. Desires, values, and outside pressures all motivate characters' actions and help to determine the story's outcome.

A Closer Look at Shakespeare

In Shakespeare's time, plays were acted for both the upper class and nobles as well as the lower class and illiterate citizens. Shakespeare's plays can be classified in three genres: tragedy, history, and comedy. Tragedy deals with great suffering and distraction and usually ends with the death of the main character. Shakespeare's history plays are based on the lives of English Kings. Comedy is a play intended to make the audience laugh, results in marriage, and the protagonist usually ends up better than he started out.

This book includes the following titles:

- *Twelfth Night*—Act I, Scene II
- *Julius Caesar*—Act I, Scene I
- *The Tempest*—Act I, Scene I
- *Henry V*—Act IV, Scene III
- *Othello*—Act I, Scene III
- *Richard III*—Act I, Scene I
- *Winter's Tale*—Act II, Scene II
- *Hamlet*—Act IV, Scene VII
- *King Lear*—Act I, Scene I
- *Macbeth*—Act I, Scene VII
- *Much Ado About Nothing*—Act II, Scene III
- *The Merchant of Venice*—Act V, Scene I
- *A Midsummer Night's Dream*—Act II, Scene I
- *Romeo and Juliet*—Act II, Scene II
- *The Taming of the Shrew*—Act II, Scene I

A Closer Look at Shakespeare *(cont.)*

The table below characterizes the passages by element. However, all of the selected passages *can* present multiple elements.

Element of Fiction	Passage Title
Setting	• Excerpt from *Twelfth Night*—Act I, Scene II • Excerpt from *Julius Caesar*—Act I, Scene I • Excerpt from *The Tempest*—Act I, Scene I
Character	• Excerpt from *Henry V*—Act IV, Scene III • Excerpt from *Othello*—Act I, Scene III • Excerpt from *Richard III*—Act I, Scene I • Excerpt from *Winter's Tale*—Act II, Scene II
Plot	• Excerpt from *Hamlet*—Act IV, Scene VII • Excerpt from *King Lear*—Act I, Scene I • Excerpt from *Macbeth*—Act I, Scene VII • Excerpt from *Much Ado About Nothing*—Act II, Scene III
Language Usage	• Excerpt from *The Merchant of Venice*—Act V, Scene I • Excerpt from *A Midsummer Night's Dream*—Act II, Scene I • Excerpt from *Romeo and Juliet*—Act II, Scene II • Excerpt from *The Taming of the Shrew*—Act II, Scene I

Leveled Texts to Differentiate Instruction

Today's classrooms contain diverse pools of learners. Above-level, on-level, below-level, and English language learners all come together to learn from one teacher in one classroom. The teacher is expected to meet their diverse needs. These students have different learning styles, come from different cultures, experience a variety of emotions, and have varied interests. And, they differ in academic readiness when it comes to reading. At times, the challenges teachers face can be overwhelming as they struggle to create learning environments that address the differences in their students while at the same time ensure that all students master the required grade-level objectives.

What is differentiation? Tomlinson and Imbau say, "Differentiation is simply a teacher attending to the learning needs of a particular student or small group of students, rather than teaching a class as though all individuals in it were basically alike" (2010). Any teacher who keeps learners at the forefront of his or her instruction can successfully provide differentiation. The effective teacher asks, "What am I going to do to shape instruction to meet the needs of all my learners?" One method or methodology will not reach all students.

Differentiation includes what is taught, how it is taught, and the products students create to show what they have learned. When differentiating curriculum, teachers become organizers of learning opportunities within the classroom environment. These opportunities are often referred to as *content*, *process*, and *product*.

- **Content:** Differentiating the content means to put more depth into the curriculum through organizing the curriculum concepts and structure of knowledge.

- **Process:** Differentiating the process requires using varied instructional techniques and materials to enhance student learning.

- **Product:** Cognitive development and students' abilities to express themselves improves when products are differentiated.

Leveled Texts to Differentiate Instruction (cont.)

Teachers should differentiate by content, process, and product according to students' differences. These differences include student *readiness*, *learning styles*, and *interests*.

- **Readiness:** If a learning experience aligns closely with students' previous skills and understanding of a topic, they will learn better.

- **Learning styles:** Teachers should create assignments that allow students to complete work according to their personal preferences and styles.

- **Interests:** If a topic sparks excitement in the learners, then students will become involved in learning and better remember what is taught.

Typically, reading teachers select different novels or texts that are leveled for their classrooms because only one book may either be too difficult or too easy for a particular group of students. One group of students will read one novel while another group reads another, and so on. What makes *Leveled Texts for Classic Fiction: Shakespeare* unique is that all students, regardless of reading level, can read the same selection from a story and can participate in whole-class discussions about it. This is possible because each selection is leveled at four different reading levels to accommodate students' reading abilities. Regardless of the reading level, all of the selections present the same content. Teachers can then focus on the same content standard or objective for the whole class, but individual students can access the content at their particular instructional levels rather than their frustration level and avoid the frustration of a selection at too high or low a level.

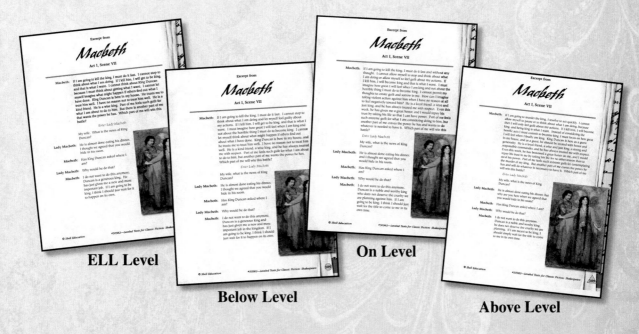

ELL Level

Below Level

On Level

Above Level

Leveled Texts to Differentiate Instruction *(cont.)*

Teachers should use the texts in this series to scaffold the content for their students. At the beginning of the year, students at the lowest reading levels may need focused teacher guidance. As the year progresses, teachers can begin giving students multiple levels of the same text to allow them to work independently at improving their comprehension. This means that each student will have a copy of the text at his or her independent reading level and at the instructional reading level. As students read the instructional-level texts, they can use the lower-leveled texts to better understand difficult vocabulary. By scaffolding the content in this way, teachers can support students as they move up through the reading levels and encourage them to work with texts that are closer to the grade level at which they will be tested.

A teacher does not need to draw attention to the fact that the texts are leveled. Nor should they hide it. Teachers who want students to read the text together can use homogeneous groups and distribute the texts after students join the groups. Or, teachers can distribute copies of the appropriate level to each student by copying the pages and separating them by each level.

Teaching Suggestions

Strategies for Higher-Order Thinking

Open-ended questions are a great way to infuse higher-order thinking skills into instruction. Open-ended questions have many appropriate answers and are exclusively dependent on the creativity of the student. Rarely do these questions have only one correct answer. It is up to the students to think and decide on their own what the answer should be. This is critical thinking at its very best. The following are some characteristics of open-ended questions:

- They ask students to *think* and *reflect*.
- They ask students to provide their *feelings* and *opinions*.
- They make students responsible for the *control* of the conversation.

There are many reasons to prefer open-ended over closed-ended questions. First, students must know the facts of the story to answer open-ended questions. Any higher-order question by necessity will encompass lower-order, fact-based questions. For a student to be able to answer a *what if* question (which is an example of an open-ended question), he or she must know the content of the story (which is a lower-level fact).

Open-ended questions also stimulate students to go beyond typical questions about a text. They spark real conversations about a text and are enriching. As a result, more students will be eager to participate in class discussions. In a more dynamic atmosphere, students will naturally make outside connections to the text, and there will be no need to force such connections.

Some students may at first be resistant to open-ended questions because they are afraid to think creatively. Years of looking for the one correct answer may make many students fear failure and embarrassment if they get the "wrong" answer. It will take time for these students to feel at ease with these questions. Model how to answer such questions. Keep encouraging students to answer them. Most importantly, be patient. The following are some examples of open-ended questions:

- Why do you think the author selected this setting?

- What are some explanations for the character's decisions?
- What are some lessons that this passage can teach us?
- How do the words set the mood or tone of this passage?

Teaching Suggestions (cont.)

Strategies for Higher-Order Thinking (cont.)

The tables below and on the following page are examples of open-ended questions and question stems that are specific to the elements of fiction covered in this series. Choose questions to challenge students to think more deeply about specific elements.

Setting
• In what ways did the setting…
• Describe the ways in which the author used setting to…
• What if the setting changed to…
• What are some possible explanations for selecting this setting?
• What would be a better setting for this story, and why is it better?
• Why did the author select this setting?
• What new element would you add to this setting to make it better?
• Explain several reasons why the characters fit well in this setting.
• Explain several reasons why the characters might fit better in a new setting.
• What makes this setting predictable or unpredictable?
• What setting would make the story more exciting? Explain.
• What setting would make the story dull? Explain.
• Why is the setting important to the story?

Character
• What is the likelihood that the character will…
• Form a hypothesis about what might happen to the character if…
• In what ways did the character show his/her thoughts by his/her actions?
• How might you have done this differently than the character?
• What are some possible explanations for the character's decisions about…
• Explain several reasons why the characters fit well in this setting.
• Explain several reasons why the characters don't fit well in this setting.
• What are some ways you would improve this character's description?
• Predict what the character will do next. Explain.
• What makes this character believable?
• For what reasons do you like or dislike this character?
• What makes this character memorable?
• What is the character thinking?

Teaching Suggestions *(cont.)*

Strategies for Higher-Order Thinking *(cont.)*

Plot

- How does this event affect…
- Predict the outcome…
- What other outcomes could have been possible, and why?
- What problems does this create?
- What is the likelihood…
- Propose a solution.
- Form a hypothesis.
- What is the theme of this story?
- What is the moral of this story?
- What lessons could this story teach us?
- How is this story similar to other stories you have read?
- How is this story similar to other movies you have watched?
- What sequel could result from this story?

Language Usage

- Describe the ways in which the author used language to…
- In what ways did language usage…
- What is the best description of…
- How would you have described this differently?
- What is a better way of describing this, and what makes it better?
- How can you improve upon the word selection…
- How can you improve upon the description of…
- What other words could be substituted for…
- What pictures do the words paint in your mind?
- How do the words set the mood or tone?
- Why would the author decide to use…
- What are some comparisons you could add to…
- In what ways could you add exaggeration to this sentence?

Teaching Suggestions *(cont.)*

Reading Strategies for Literature

The college and career readiness anchor standards within the Common Core State Standards in reading (National Governors Association Center for Best Practices and Council of Chief State School Officers 2010) include understanding key ideas and details, recognizing craft and structure, and being able to integrate knowledge and ideas. The following two pages offer practical strategies for achieving these standards using the texts found in this book.

Identifying Key Ideas and Details

- Have students work together to create talking tableaux based on parts of the text that infer information. A tableau is a freeze-frame where students are asked to pose and explain the scene from the text they are depicting. As students stand still, they take turns breaking away from the tableau to tell what is being inferred at that moment and how they know this. While this strategy is good for all students, it is a strong activity for **English language learners** because they have an opportunity for encoding and decoding with language and actions.

- Theme is the lesson that the story teaches its readers. It can be applied to everyone, not just the characters in the story. Have students identify the theme and write about what happens that results in their conclusions. Ask students to make connections as to how they can apply the theme to their lives. Allow **below-grade-level** writers to record this information, use graphic organizers for structure, or illustrate their answers in order to make the information more concrete for them.

- Have students draw a picture of the character during an important scene in the story, and use thought bubbles to show the character's secret thoughts based on specific details found in the text. This activity can benefit everyone, but it is very effective for **below-grade-level** writers and **English language learners**. Offering students an opportunity to draw their answers provides them with a creative method to communicate their ideas.

- Have students create before-and-after pictures that show how the characters change over the course of the story. Encourage **above-grade-level** students to examine characters' personality traits and how the characters' thoughts change. This activity encourages students to think about the rationale behind the personality traits they assigned to each character.

Teaching Suggestions (cont.)

Reading Strategies for Literature (cont.)

Understanding Craft and Structure

- Ask students to identify academic vocabulary in the texts and to practice using the words in a meet-and-greet activity in the classroom, walking around and having conversations using them. This gives **English language learners** an opportunity to practice language acquisition in an authentic way.

- Have students create mini-posters that display the figurative language used in the story. This strategy encourages **below-grade-level** students to show what they have learned.

- Allow students to work in pairs to draw sets of stairs on large paper, and then write how each part of the story builds on the previous part and fits together to provide the overall structure of the story. Homogeneously partner students so that **above-grade-level** students will challenge one another.

- Select at least two or three texts, and have students compare the point of view from which the different stories are narrated. Then, have students change the point of view (e.g., if the story is written in first person, have students rewrite a paragraph in third person). This is a challenging activity specifically suited for **on-grade-level** and **above-grade-level** students to stimulate higher-order thinking.

- Pose the following questions to students: What if the story is told from a different point of view? How does that change the story? Have students select another character's point of view and brainstorm lists of possible changes. This higher-order thinking activity is open-ended and effective for **on-level**, **above-level**, **below-level**, and **English language learners**.

Integrating Knowledge and Ideas

- Show students a section from a movie, a play, or a reader's theater about the story. Have students use graphic organizers to compare and contrast parts of the text with scenes from one of these other sources. Such visual displays support comprehension for **below-level** and **English language learners**.

- Have students locate several illustrations in the text, and then rate the illustrations based on their effective visuals. This higher-order thinking activity is open-ended and is great for **on-level**, **below-level**, **above-level**, and **English language learners**.

- Let students create playlists of at least five songs to go with the mood and tone of the story. Then instruct students to give an explanation for each chosen song. Musically inclined students tend to do very well with this type of activity. It also gives a reason for writing, which can engage **below-grade-level** writers.

- Have students partner up to create talk show segments that discuss similar themes found in the story. Each segment should last between one and two minutes and can be performed live or taped. Encourage students to use visuals, props, and other tools to make it real. Be sure to homogeneously group students for this activity and aid your **below-level** students so they can be successful. This activity allows for **all students** to bring their creative ideas to the table and positively contribute to the end result.

Teaching Suggestions (cont.)

Fiction as a Model for Writing

It is only natural that reading and writing go hand in hand in students' literacy development. Both are important for functioning in the real world as adults. Established pieces of fiction, like the ones in this book, serve as models for how to write effectively. After students read the texts in this book, take time for writing instruction. Below are some ideas for writing mini-lessons that can be taught using the texts from this book as writing exemplars.

How to Begin Writing a Story

Instead of beginning a story with 'Once upon a time' or 'Long, long ago,' teach students to mimic the styles of well-known authors. As students begin writing projects, show them a variety of first sentences or paragraphs written by different authors. Discuss how these selections are unique. Encourage students to change or adapt the types of beginnings found in the models to make their own story hooks.

Using Good Word Choice

Good word choice can make a significant difference in writing. Help students paint vivid word pictures by showing them examples within the passages found in this book. Instead of writing *I live in a beautiful house*, students can write *I live in a yellow-framed house with black shutters and white pillars that support the wraparound porch.* Encourage students to understand that writing is enriched with sensory descriptions that include what the characters smell, hear, taste, touch, and see. Make students aware of setting the emotional tone in their stories. For example, *In an instant, the hair on the back of his neck stood up, the door creaked open, and a hand reached through.* This example sets a scary mood. Hyperbole is also a great tool to use for effect in stories.

Character Names Can Have Meaning

Students can use names to indicate clues about their characters' personalities. Mrs. Strict could be a teacher, Dr. Molar could be a dentist, and Butch could be the class bully. Remind students that the dialogue between their characters should be real, not forced. Students should think about how people really talk and write dialogue using jargon and colorful words, for example, *"Hey you little twerp, come back here!" yelled Brutus.*

How to Use This Book

Classroom Management for Leveled Texts

Determining your students' instructional reading levels is the first step in the process of effectively managing the leveled-text passages. It is important to assess their reading abilities often so they do not get stuck on one level. Below are suggested ways to use this resource, as well as other resources available to you, to determine students' reading levels.

Running records: While your class is doing independent work, pull your below-grade-level students aside one at a time. Have them individually read aloud the lowest level of a text (the star level) as you record any errors they make on your own copy of the text. Assess their accuracy and fluency, mark the words they say incorrectly, and listen for fluent reading. Use your judgment to determine whether students seem frustrated as they read. If students read accurately and fluently and comprehend the material, move them up to the next level and repeat the process. Following the reading, ask comprehension questions to assess their understanding of the material. As a general guideline, students reading below 90 percent accuracy are likely to feel frustrated as they read. A variety of other published reading assessment tools are available to assess students' reading levels with the running-records format.

Refer to other resources: Another way to determine instructional reading levels is to check your students' Individualized Education Plans; ask the school's language development specialists and/or special education teachers; or review test scores. All of these resources can provide the additional information needed to determine students' reading levels.

How to Use This Book *(cont.)*

Distributing the Texts

Some teachers wonder about how to distribute the different-leveled texts within the classroom. They worry that students will feel insulted or insecure if they do not get the same material as their neighbors. Prior to distributing the texts, make sure that the classroom environment is one in which all students learn at their individual instructional levels. It is important to make this clear. Otherwise, students may constantly ask why their work is different from another student's work. Simply state that students will not be working on the same assignment every day and that their work may slightly vary to resolve students' curiosity. In this approach, distribution of the texts can be very open and causal, just like passing out any other assignment.

Teachers who would rather not have students aware of the differences in the texts can try the suggestions below:

- Make a pile in your hands from star to triangle. Put your finger between the circle and square levels. As you approach each student, pull from the top (star), above your finger (circle), below your finger (square), or the bottom (triangle), depending on each student's level. If you do not hesitate too much in front of each desk, students will probably not notice.

- Begin the class period with an opening activity. Put the texts in different places around the room. As students work quietly, circulate and direct students to the right locations for retrieving the texts you want them to use.

- Organize the texts in small piles by seating arrangement so that when you arrive at a group of desks, you will have only the levels you need.

How to Use This Book (cont.)

Components of the Product

Each passage is derived from classic literary selections. Classics expose readers to cultural heritage or the literature of a culture. Classics improve understanding of the past and, in turn, understanding of the present. These selections from the past explain how we got to where we are today.

The Levels

There are 15 passages in this book, each from a different work of classic fiction. Each passage is leveled to four different reading levels. The images and fonts used for each level within a work of fiction look the same.

1.5–2.2   3.0–3.5

Behind each page number, you will see a shape. These shapes indicate the reading levels of each piece so that you can make sure students are working with the correct texts. The chart on the following page provides specific levels of each text.

5.0–5.5   6.5–3.5

Leveling Process

The texts in this series are excerpts from classic pieces of literature. A reading specialist has reviewed each excerpt and leveled each one to create four distinct reading passages with unique levels.

Elements of Fiction Question

Each text includes one comprehension question that directs the students to think about the chosen element of fiction for that passage. These questions are written at the appropriate reading level to allow all students to successfully participate in a whole-class discussion. These questions are open-ended and designed to stimulate higher-order thinking.

Digital Resource CD

The Digital Resource CD allows for easy access to all the reading passages in this book. Electronic PDF files as well as word files are included on the CD.

How to Use This Book (cont.)

Title	ELL Level ★ 1.5–2.2	Below Level ● 3.0–3.5	On level ■ 5.0–5.5	Above level ▲ 6.5–7.2
Setting Passages				
Twelfth Night—Act I, Scene II	2.2	3.3	5.3	6.5
Julius Caesar—Act I, Scene I	2.2	3.2	5.1	6.5
The Tempest—Act I, Scene I	2.2	3.0	5.0	6.5
Character Passages				
Henry V—Act VI, Scene III	2.2	3.0	5.0	6.5
Othello—Act I, Scene III	2.2	3.5	5.0	6.5
Richard III—Act I, Scene I	2.2	3.5	5.5	6.8
The Winter's Tale—Act II, Scene II	2.2	3.4	5.4	6.5
Plot Passages				
Hamlet—Act IV, Scene VII	2.2	3.5	5.0	6.5
King Lear—Act I, Scene I	2.2	3.5	5.1	6.7
Macbeth—Act I, Scene VII	2.0	3.5	5.0	6.5
Much Ado About Nothing—Act II, Scene III	2.2	3.2	5.5	6.5
Language Usage Passages				
The Merchant of Venice—Act V, Scene I	2.2	3.2	5.0	6.7
A Midsummer Night's Dream—Act II, Scene I	2.2	3.5	5.5	6.5
Romeo and Juliet—Act II, Scene II	2.0	3.5	5.4	6.7
The Taming of the Shrew—Act II, Scene I	1.5	3.0	5.0	6.5

Correlations to Standards

Shell Education is committed to producing educational materials that are research and standards based. In this effort, we have correlated all our products to the academic standards of all 50 United States, the District of Columbia, the Department of Defense Dependent Schools, and all Canadian provinces.

How to Find Standards Correlations

To print a customized correlations report of this product for your state, visit our website at **http://www.shelleducation.com** and follow the on-screen directions. If you require assistance in printing correlations reports, please contact Customer Service at 1-800-858-7339.

Purpose and Intent of Standards

Legislation mandates that all states adopt academic standards that identify the skills students will learn in kindergarten through grade twelve. Many states also have standards for pre-K. This same legislation sets requirements to ensure the standards are detailed and comprehensive.

Standards are designed to focus instruction and guide adoption of curricula. Standards are statements that describe the criteria necessary for students to meet specific academic goals. They define the knowledge, skills, and content students should acquire at each level. Standards are also used to develop standardized tests to evaluate students' academic progress.

Teachers are required to demonstrate how their lessons meet state standards. State standards are used in the development of all our products, so educators can be assured they meet the academic requirements of each state.

McREL Compendium

We use the Mid-continent Research for Education and Learning (McREL) Compendium to create standards correlations. Each year, McREL analyzes state standards and revises the compendium. By following this procedure, McREL is able to produce a general compilation of national standards. Each lesson in this product is based on one or more McREL standards. The chart on the following pages lists each standard taught in this product and the page numbers for the corresponding lessons.

TESOL Standards

The lessons in this book promote English language development for English language learners. The standards listed on the following pages support the language objectives presented throughout the lessons.

Common Core State Standards

The texts in this book are aligned to the Common Core State Standards (CCSS). The standards correlation can be found on pages 28–29.

Correlations to Standards *(cont.)*

Correlation to Common Core State Standards

The passages in this book are aligned to the Common Core State Standards (CCSS). Students who meet these standards develop the skills in reading that are the foundation for any creative and purposeful expression in language.

Grade(s)	Standard
3	RL.3.10—By the end of year, independently and proficiently read and comprehend literature, including stories, dramas, and poetry, at the high end of the grades 2–3 text-complexity band
4–5	RL.4.10–5.10—By the end of the year, proficiently read and comprehend literature, including stories, dramas, and poetry, in the grades 4–5 text-complexity band, with scaffolding as needed at the high end of the range
6–8	RL.6.10–8.10—By the end of the year, proficiently read and comprehend literature, including stories, dramas, and poems, in the grades 6–8 text-complexity band, with scaffolding as needed at the high end of the range.

As outlined by the Common Core State Standards, teachers are "free to provide students with whatever tools and knowledge their professional judgment and experience identify as most helpful for meeting the goals set out in the standards." Bearing this in mind, teachers are encouraged to use the recommendations indicated in the chart below in order to meet additional CCSS Reading Standards that require further instruction.

Standard	Additional Instruction
RL.3.1–5.1— Key Ideas and Details	• Ask and answer questions to demonstrate understanding of a text. • Refer to details and examples in a text. • Quote accurately from a text when explaining what the text says.
RL.3.2–5.2— Key Ideas and Details	• Recount stories to determine the central message, lesson, or moral and explain how it is conveyed. • Determine a theme of a story from details in the text.
RL.3.3–5.3— Key Ideas and Details	• Describe in depth a character, setting, or event in a story.
RL.6.1–8.1— Key Ideas and Details	• Cite textual evidence to support analysis of what the text says.
RL.6.2–8.2— Key Ideas and Details	• Determine a theme or central idea of a text and analyze its development over the course of the text.
RL.6.3–8.3— Key Ideas and Details	• Analyze how particular elements of a story or drama interact.

Correlations to Standards *(cont.)*

Correlation to Common Core State Standards *(cont.)*

Standard	Additional Instruction *(cont.)*
RL.3.4–8.4— Craft and Structure	• Determine the meaning of words and phrases as they are used in the text.
RL.3.5–5.5— Craft and Structure	• Refer to parts of stories when writing or speaking about a text. • Explain the overall structure of a story.
RL.3.6–8.6— Craft and Structure	• Distinguish and describe point of view within the story.
RL.6.5–8.5— Craft and Structure	• Analyze and compare and contrast the overall structure of a story.
RL.3.7–5.7— Integration of Knowledge and Ideas	• Explain how specific aspects of a text's illustrations contribute to what is conveyed by the words in a story.
RL.3.9–8.9— Integration of Knowledge and Ideas	• Compare and contrast the themes, settings, and plots of stories.

Correlation to McREL Standards

Standard	Page(s)
5.1—Previews text (3–5)	all
5.1—Establishes and adjusts purposes for reading (6–8)	all
5.2—Establishes and adjusts purposes for reading (3–5)	all
5.3—Makes, confirms, and revises simple predictions about what will be found in a text (3–5)	all
5.3—Uses a variety of strategies to extend reading vocabulary (6–8)	all
5.4—Uses specific strategies to clear up confusing parts of a text (6–8)	all
5.5—Use a variety of context clues to decode unknown words (3–5)	all
5.5—Understands specific devices an author uses to accomplish his or her purpose (6–8)	all
5.6—Reflects on what has been learned after reading and formulates ideas, opinions, and personal responses to texts (6–8)	all

Correlation to Standards (cont.)

Correlation to McREL Standards (cont.)

Standard	Page(s)
5.7—Understands level-appropriate reading vocabulary (3–5)	all
5.8—Monitors own reading strategies and makes modifications as needed (3–5)	all
5.10—Understands the author's purpose or point of view (3–5)	all
6.1—Reads a variety of literary passages and texts (3–5, 6–8)	all
6.2—Knows the defining characteristics and structural elements of a variety of literary genres (3–5, 6–8)	all
6.3—Understands the basic concept of plot (3–5)	all
6.3—Understands complex elements of plot development (6–8)	all
6.4—Understands similarities and differences within and among literary works from various genres and cultures (3–5)	all
6.4—Understands elements of character development (6–8)	all
6.5—Understands elements of character development in literary works (3–5)	all
6.7—Understands the ways in which language is used in literary texts (3–5)	all

Correlation to TESOL Standards

Standard	Page(s)
2.1—Students will use English to interact in the classroom	all
2.2—Students will use English to obtain, process, construct, and provide subject matter information in spoken and written form	all
2.3—Students will use appropriate learning strategies to construct and apply academic knowledge	all

Excerpt from

Twelfth Night

Act I, Scene II

Viola: What country are we in?

Captain: This country is called Illyria.

Viola: What am I going to do here? I see that my brother is not here. Our ship was sailing to another country. Do you think there is a chance he drowned?

Captain: You should feel lucky to be safe and alive. The storm was dangerous.

Viola: My poor, wonderful brother. I hope that he lives, wherever he is.

Captain: I hope so. I do believe that after our ship was broken into pieces, I saw your brother. He was holding tightly to some boards of the ship. You need to have faith and believe that he was able to make it safely through the waves.

Viola: Thank you for saying that. Do you know anything about this place?

Captain: I do. I was born and raised about three hours away from here.

Viola: Who is the ruler here?

Captain: A wonderful and kind duke.

Viola: What is his name?

Captain: Orsino.

Viola: Orsino! I have heard my father talk about him. Is he married?

Captain: No, not that I have heard. I do know that he has loved a beautiful woman named Olivia for a long time.

Viola: Do you know anything about her?

Captain: She is a wonderful lady. Her father was a count. He died about a year ago. He left his other child, a son, in charge of Olivia. He died soon after his father. In the sadness of all that death, Olivia has gone into hiding. She refuses to see or talk with any men at all.

Viola: She is a lucky woman to be able to choose whom she does and does not want to talk with. I wish that I could have such choices in my own life.

Captain: It may seem nice on the outside, but she must be lonely. She will not allow any man near her. Not even the duke.

Viola: You may look rough and worn on the outside. But on the inside, you are a good and kind man. I will now ask for your help. I will pay you well for any help that you can give me. I will work for this duke. I will need to be dressed as a boy. I will need you to introduce me as a boy. Will you help me and keep this secret that I am really a girl?

Captain: I will keep silent with this secret.

Viola: Thank you, Captain. Let us go to find the duke.

Element Focus: Setting

Why did the author select this setting?

Excerpt from

Twelfth Night

Act I, Scene II

◇◇◇

Viola: My good friend, what country is this?

Captain: We are in Illyria, my lady.

Viola: What are we doing in Illyria? Our ship was supposed to go to another country. What has happened to my brother? Do you think he has drowned in the waves?

Captain: You should be calm and grateful that you are safe and alive.

Viola: Oh, my brother. Perhaps he was able to make it to safety as well.

Captain: Yes, my lady, I believe that he might still be alive. After our ship was tattered into pieces from the waves, I believe that I saw your brother holding tightly to some of the floating boards from our ship. Perhaps the currents have transported him to another place where he has landed without harm.

Viola: Thank you for saying so. Do you know this place upon which we have landed, Captain?

Captain: Yes. I was born and raised about three hours away from here.

Viola: And who is the ruler here?

Captain: A wonderful duke.

Viola: What is this duke's name?

Captain: Orsino.

Viola: Orsino! I have heard my father mention a duke named Orsino. He is unmarried, if I remember my father's stories correctly.

Captain: Yes, my lady, he is unmarried although not by choice. For a long time, he has loved a gentle woman named Olivia.

Viola: Who is she?

Captain: A beautiful and caring young woman. Her father died about a year ago and left her brother to take care of her. But that brother died soon after. And ever since those two deaths, she has been so overcome with sadness that she will not speak to or see any men.

Viola: How fortunate she is to be able to choose her own path. I wish that I could speak for myself and not be told what to do.

Captain: But that freedom must make her lonely. She will allow no man near her. Not even the duke.

Viola: Although you may look harsh and mean on the outside, your heart on the inside is generous. I would like to ask for your help. I will work for this duke, but I must keep myself safe. In order to do this, I ask that you help me by dressing me as a boy. Then, when we go to the duke, you will present me as a boy and never tell that you know I am a girl. I will pay you well for keeping this secret. Will you help me?

Captain: My mouth will remain silent with your secret.

Viola: Thank you. Now let us find that duke.

Element Focus: Setting

Why is the setting important to the story?

Excerpt from

Twelfth Night

Act I, Scene II

Viola: My good friend, what country is this in which we have landed?

Captain: We are in Illyria, my lady.

Viola: What are we doing in Illyria when our ship was supposed to go to another country? And what has happened to my brother? Do you think he has drowned in the crashing waves?

Captain: You should be thankful that you have been able to discover yourself securely on land after that appalling storm.

Viola: What could have possibly happened to my wonderful brother? Perhaps he was able to find his way safely to another shore.

Captain: Yes, my lady, you should feel confident that he might still be alive. As the storm raged, I saw our ship being torn apart in the waves. I believe that I saw your brother clinging to some of the abandoned boards. Perhaps the currents have transported him to another place where he has landed without harm.

Viola: You are a gentleman for saying so. Do you know this place upon which we have landed, Captain?

Captain: Yes, my lady. I was born and raised about three hours away from here.

Viola: And who is the ruler here?

Captain: A wonderful duke.

Viola: What is this duke's name?

Captain: Orsino.

Viola: Orsino! I recollect my father mentioning a duke named Orsino. He is unmarried, if I can recall my father's stories accurately.

Captain: Yes, my lady, although his status as a single man is not by choice. For as long as I have known him, he has loved a gentle woman named Olivia.

Viola: Who is this Olivia?

Captain: A beautiful and generous woman whose father died just this year. After his death, he left her brother to care for her, but he tragically died soon after her father. Ever since those deaths, she has become overwhelmed with depression and will not communicate with or see any men.

Viola: How fortunate she is to be able to regulate her own path. I wish I had the authority to speak for myself and not simply be expected to obey.

Captain: But she must be very secluded, for in that freedom to communicate for herself, she has closed herself away from all men, even the duke.

Viola: Although you may look harsh on the outside, on the inside you are an honorable and trustworthy man with a temperate heart. I will work for this duke, but I must keep myself safe, and for that, I need your assistance. Firstly, I must be dressed as a boy—in clothing that will not give away that I am female. Then, when we go to the duke, you will introduce me to him as a boy servant and never reveal that you know I am a girl. I will pay you well for protecting this secret. Will you assist me?

Captain: My mouth will remain inaudible with your secret.

Viola: Thank you; now let us locate that duke.

Element Focus: Setting

What are some possible explanations for selecting this setting?

Excerpt from

Twelfth Night

Act I, Scene II

◇◇

Viola: My good friend, what country is this where we have found ourselves?

Captain: We are in the country of Illyria, my lady.

Viola: What are we doing in Illyria when our ship was bound for another country entirely? Do you think that my brother has drowned in the dangerous waves of this unpleasant storm?

Captain: You should compose yourself and be thankful that you have been able to discover yourself securely on dry land after the frightening lashing our ship received.

Viola: What can you imagine has happened to my wonderful brother? Perhaps he was strong enough to tolerate the rough and tumultuous ocean and is now breathing the fresh air of another shore.

Captain: Yes, my lady, you should maintain confidence that your brother is alive. As the storm blustered against us, I saw our ship being torn apart in the waves, and I believe I remember seeing your brother clinging tightly to some of the abandoned boards. Perhaps the currents have transported him, still alive, to another shore where he has landed without harm and awaits finding you.

Viola: You are a noble and honorable gentleman for saying so. Do you distinguish this place upon which we have landed, Captain?

Captain: Yes, my lady, I recognize it very well, as I was born and raised about three hours away from here.

Viola: And who is the ruler here in your homeland?

Captain: A wonderful duke who is upright and just in both actions and name.

Viola: And what is this duke's name?

Captain: Orsino.

Viola: Orsino! I recall my father mentioning a duke named Orsino in his stories to me. If I can recall my father's stories correctly, this duke, Orsino, is not married. Do I have that accurate?

Captain: Yes, my lady, although his status as a single man is not of his own choice. For as long as I have known him, he has loved Olivia.

Viola: Who is this Olivia?

Captain: A beautiful and generous woman whose father died just this year. After his death, he left her brother to care for her, but he tragically died soon after. Ever since those deaths, she has become depressed and will not communicate with or see any men.

Viola: How fortunate she is to be able to regulate her own path. I wish I had the authority to communicate for myself and not simply be expected to obey.

Captain: But she must be very secluded, for in that freedom to communicate for herself, she has closed herself away from all men—even the duke.

Viola: Although you may look harsh on the exterior, you are an honorable and trustworthy man with a gentle heart on the inside. I have decided that I will work for this duke, but I will need your assistance. Firstly, I must be dressed as a boy. Then, you will introduce me to the duke as a boy servant and never reveal to anyone that you know I am a girl. I will recompense you well for maintaining this secret. Will you assist me?

Captain: My mouth will remain inaudible with your secret.

Viola: Thank you; now let us locate that duke.

Element Focus: Setting

Explain several reasons why the main character fits well with this setting.

Excerpt from

Julius Caesar

Act I, Scene I

Flavius: You lazy man! Get away from me now! Do you think that today is a day off? I can see from your clothes that you are not a rich man. What is your normal job?

First Commoner: I am a carpenter, sir.

Marullus: Then, where are your tools? You look like you are wearing your best clothes. Why is that? You, over there, what is your normal job?

Second Commoner: I am a shoemaker, sir.

Marullus: I do not understand. Answer me, now. What is your job?

Second Commoner: I fix the bottom of people's shoes. It is so they can walk correctly.

Marullus: Are you trying to make me angry? What would a poor man like you know about walking correctly?

Second Commoner: You do not need to be upset with me. I can fix whatever is getting in the way of your path.

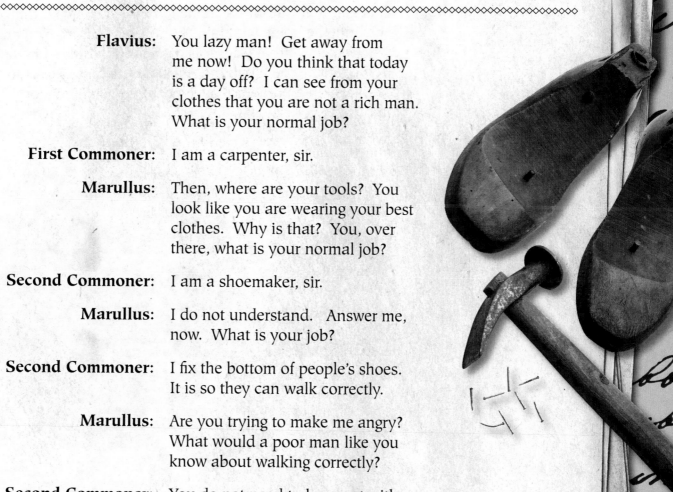

Marullus: I think you are trying to make fun of me. I will not have that!

Flavius: Enough of this. Why aren't you in your store today? What are you doing out here in the street?

Second Commoner: Today is a holiday for everyone. Caesar is returning as a winner from his battles. We are here to celebrate him.

Marullus: What is it that Caesar has done to help you? What things is he bringing home with him to show his power? You are dumb to believe that Caesar is good for anything. I have watched you. You climb the walls of buildings to wait to see Caesar in a parade. I have heard you cheering for him. Don't you see that you are being happy because of another person's pain? When you celebrate a win for Caesar, you also celebrate a loss for someone else. Get out of this street and go home. Find somewhere else to behave like rude men.

Element Focus: Setting

What kind of people are out on the street in this passage? Why do you think they are there?

Excerpt from

Julius Caesar

Act I, Scene I

Flavius:	Get away from me, you lazy man! Do you think that today is a day off? I can see from your clothes that you are not a wealthy man. What is your regular job?
First Commoner:	I am a carpenter, sir.
Marullus:	Then, where are your tools and the things that help you work? You look like you are wearing your best clothes. Why is that? You, over there, what is your regular job?
Second Commoner:	I am a shoemaker, sir.
Marullus:	I do not understand. Now answer me, what is your job?
Second Commoner:	I fix the bottom of people's shoes. It is so they can walk correctly in their lives.
Marullus:	Are you trying to make me angry? What would a deprived man like you know about walking correctly?
Second Commoner:	You do not need to be upset with me. I promise you that I can repair whatever is getting in the way of your path.

Marullus: I think you are trying to make fun of me.
I will not have that!

Flavius: Enough of this. Why aren't you in your store today?
What are you doing out here in the crowded street?

Second Commoner: Today is a holiday for everyone. Caesar is returning as a
champion from his battles, and we are here to celebrate
him.

Marullus: What is it that Caesar has done to bring you such joy?
What things is he bringing home with him to show his
power? You are dumb to believe that Caesar is good
for anything. I have watched you climb the walls of
buildings to wait to see Caesar in a parade. I have heard
your cheering and
yells of joy echo all
around the buildings
of the city. Don't
you see that you are
celebrating another
person's pain? When
you celebrate a win
for Caesar, you also
celebrate a loss for
someone else. Get
out of this street
and go home. Find
somewhere else to
behave like rude and
ungrateful men.

Element Focus: Setting

What is a better setting for this
story and why is it better?

Excerpt from

Julius Caesar

Act I, Scene I

Flavius:	Get away from me, you lazy man! Do you think that today is a special holiday? I can see from your garments that you are not wealthy but are rather a working man. What is your ordinary job?
First Commoner:	I am a carpenter, sir.
Marullus:	Then, where are your tools and instruments that assist you when you work? You look like you are wearing your best clothes today. You, over there, what is your ordinary job?
Second Commoner:	I am a shoemaker, sir.
Marullus:	I do not comprehend. Answer me right now—what is your occupation?
Second Commoner:	I fix the bottom of people's shoes. It is so they can walk appropriately in their lives.
Marullus:	Are you trying to make me angry? Are you saying that there is something keeping me from being accurate in my own life? What would a deprived man like you know about walking correctly?
Second Commoner:	There is no reason to be upset with me. I promise you that I can repair whatever is getting in the way of your path in life. I can transform your shoes to assist you with walking perfectly.

Marullus: I think you are trying to make fun of me, and I will not have that from a lowly worker!

Flavius: Enough of this silliness. Why aren't you in your store today? What are you doing in the crowded and rowdy street?

Second Commoner: Today is a holiday for everyone, rich and poor alike. Caesar is returning from his battles today as a champion, and all the people of his city have come into the street to joyously welcome him home.

Marullus: What is it that Caesar has done in these bloody battles to bring you such joy? What astounding items from faraway lands is he bringing home with him to display his power? You are ignorant fools to believe that Caesar cares about whatever you think. I have watched you climb the walls of buildings in anticipation of seeing the mighty Caesar. Can't you see that you are celebrating another person's pain? When you celebrate a win for Caesar, you also celebrate a loss for someone else. Get out of this street now. Go away and find somewhere else to behave like impolite and ungrateful men.

Element Focus: Setting

How do Marullus and Flavius not fit into the setting?

#50982—*Leveled Texts for Classic Fiction: Shakespeare*

Excerpt from

Julius Caesar

Act I, Scene I

Flavius:	Get away from me, you lazy disgusting man! Do you think that today is some kind of special holiday? I can see from your garments that you are not wealthy but are rather a working man. What is your everyday job?
First Commoner:	I am a carpenter, sir.
Marullus:	Then, where are your tools and instruments that help you work? You look like you are wearing your best clothes today and do not have your tools and instruments that help you work. I do not recall that there is anything particularly special about today. You, over there, what is your everyday job?
Second Commoner:	I am a simple shoemaker, sir.
Marullus:	I do not comprehend what you are saying. Answer me right now—what is your job every other day of the year?
Second Commoner:	I fix the bottom of people's shoes so they can walk correctly in their lives. Men should walk with their heads held high and not hung low with any pain or insincerity.
Marullus:	Are you trying to make me annoyed? Are you implying that there is something keeping me from being correct and sincere in my own life? What would a poor man like you possibly know about walking appropriately in my finely created shoes?
Second Commoner:	There is no reason for you to be troubled by me. But I promise you that I can repair whatever is getting in the way of your path in life. I can repair whatever might be hindering your step by transforming it into something that will help you walk perfectly.

Marullus: I think you are trying to make fun of me, and I will not have that from a lowly worker!

Flavius: Enough of this silliness! Sir, why aren't you in your store today fixing shoes? What are you doing out here in the crowded and rowdy street?

Second Commoner: Today is a holiday for everyone, rich and poor alike. Caesar is returning home victorious from his battles today, and all the people, lowly and powerful together, have come into the street to joyously and thankfully welcome him home.

Marullus: What is it that Caesar has done in these bloody battles to bring you such contentment? What mystical and astounding items from faraway lands is he bringing home with him to display his power? You are ignorant fools to believe that Caesar cares about your ordinary lives and what you think. I have watched you thoughtless brutes climb the walls of buildings in breathless anticipation of catching sight of the mighty Caesar. Can't you see that you are celebrating another person's pain? A win for Caesar means a disastrous and deadly loss for someone else. Get out of this street now and find somewhere else to behave like disrespectful and ungrateful men.

Element Focus: Setting

Does Marullus feel the same emotions that of people he describes the setting? Explain.

Excerpt from

The Tempest

Act I, Scene I

◇◇◇

Sebastian: Good sailor, be careful. Where is the captain?

Boatswain: You should be down below the deck. It is much safer below.

Antonio: But I need to speak with the captain. Please, tell me where he is.

Boatswain: Doing all he can to get the ship out of this storm. Now please, go. You are in the way of us being able to save the ship from the storm.

Gonzalo: No, wait. I have more to ask you.

Boatswain: Look at the size and power of the waves. This storm is harming the ship and putting our lives in danger. Please go to your cabin.

Gonzalo: Fine, I will go, but remember that you have the king on this ship.

Boatswain: I understand you are speaking for the king and trying to help. Are you powerful enough to demand the storm to move away? If so, please calm it. If not, you must get below to your cabin.

Exit

Gonzalo: I will get out of the way for now.

Enter Boatswain

Boatswain: Bring down the sail! You there! Lower, lower!

A cry within

The king and his men cry out loud like scared babies!

Enter Sebastian, Antonio, and Gonzalo

What are you doing up here? Do you want us all to drown?

Sebastian: How dare you speak to us in such a way! You are rude.

Boatswain: Down below, you can think what you want. Up here, you must work.

Antonio: You cannot tell me what to do. You are just a poor servant and we are gentlemen. We are less afraid of this horrible storm than you are.

Gonzalo: This ship is already a wreck. It is weak and has many leaks.

Boatswain: Pull the boat away from the waves. Try to steer out of the wind.

Enter Mariners, wet

Mariners: These waves and winds are strong! We will all be lost to death.

Boatswain: How can you give up now, men? We can still fight to save the ship and all aboard.

Gonzalo: The king and the prince are aboard this ship. We must help these sailors. If they go down, we go down into the sea with them.

Sebastian: This is such a waste of time.

Antonio: So you will stand there and allow these sailors to decide if we should live or die? Can you not see that we will all drown in these angry waters?

Gonzalo: But this storm does not help my plans.

A confused noise within: "Mercy on us! Farewell, my wife and children! Farewell, brother!"

Antonio: If the king dies, we must all die honorably with him.

Sebastian: No, I think we should get off this sinking ship while we can.

Exit Antonio and Sebastian

Gonzalo: I would give anything right now to be on dry ground. Let the wishes of those above us come to be. But if I could wish for it, I would want a dry death!

Element Focus: Setting

Why is this setting important to the story?

Excerpt from

The Tempest

Act I, Scene I

◇◇

Sebastian: Good sailor, please be careful. Where is the captain of this ship?

Boatswain: You should not be above deck. It is safer down below.

Antonio: I need to speak with the captain. Please inform me where he is.

Boatswain: He is doing all he can to help save all the men aboard this ship. You are keeping us from our work. Please find safety in your cabin.

Gonzalo: No, good sailor, it is important that I find and speak with the captain.

Boatswain: The waves crash against us and the wind whistles through the sails. This storm is harming our ship. Leave us to our work and go below.

Gonzalo: It would be good for you to remember the powerful royalty you have aboard this ship.

Boatswain: I understand that you are trying to speak for the king and that you want to help. Do you have an unnatural power that allows you to control these waters? If so, please use it. If not, return to your cabin.

Exit

Gonzalo: I will go below for now.

Enter Boatswain

Boatswain: Bring down the sail! Lower; bring it lower!

A cry within

These frightened men cry out like little babies!

Enter Sebastian, Antonio, and Gonzalo

What are you doing here? Do you want us carried into the ocean?

Sebastian: How dare you speak to men such as we with that rude tone!

Boatswain: Down below, you can think what you want. Up here, you must work.

Antonio: No sailor has the right to tell me what to do. We are better men. We have no fear of being taken at the watery hands of this storm.

Gonzalo: And just look at the sorry state of this ship. It leaks and cracks.

Boatswain: Pull away, men. Steer away from the waves!

Enter Mariners, wet

Mariners: We are lost to the power of these waves. We will all lose our lives.

Boatswain: How can you say that? If you believe we have no chance to survive, then we will be lost. Keep believing. We can pull through.

Gonzalo: The king and the prince are praying that we find some peace. We should go pray with them, not only for them but also for ourselves.

Sebastian: I have no patience for any of you.

Antonio: So these foolish mariners will be able to decide if we live or die? Is it not clear to you that we will drown in the heavy waters?

Gonzalo: This storm does not help my plans.

A confused noise within: "Mercy on us! Farewell, my wife and children! Farewell, brother!"

Antonio: We should all have the courage to sink with the king.

Sebastian: No, I say we get off this ship and worry about saving ourselves.

Exit Antonio and Sebastian

Gonzalo: At this moment, I would give anything for a small bit of dry land. I do know that at the end of my days, I would wish for a dry death!

Element Focus: Setting

Explain why the characters fit well in this setting.

Excerpt from

The Tempest

Act I, Scene I

◇◇◇

Sebastian: Kind mariner, where is the captain who is commander of this ship?

Boatswain: It would be best for you to remain below, for this is a frightening moment as we defend this ship from the angry storm.

Antonio: I will inquire again: Where is the captain who oversees this ship?

Boatswain: While you are above deck, you put yourself and the other men in danger. I tell you again, go to your cabin below.

Gonzalo: No, no my good mariner; it is important that you hear me out.

Boatswain: The sea, with deep and strong waves, roars against us as if it were attempting to start a fight. This water and wind does not care who you are. Now go to your cabin.

Gonzalo: Remember the significance and importance of the individuals aboard.

Boatswain: Do you have an overwhelming power that makes you able to command the forces of nature? If so, demand that the darkening sky stop pummeling into us. If not, then find safety.

Exit

Gonzalo: When we make it securely through, I will see my plan to the finale.

Enter Boatswain

Boatswain: Pull down the top sail! Bring it together with the other sails!

A cry within

Oh, these cowardly men, who cry like babies, scream out their pitiful fear!

Enter Sebastian, Antonio, and Gonzalo

Not again; I ordered you to remain below. Is it your aspiration that we sink?

Sebastian: Who gives you the authority to speak to us in such a way?

Boatswain: So be it; if you choose to stay above deck, then you must work.

Antonio: Your rudeness toward us may get you in trouble, mariner. Besides, unlike you, we have no horror of being carried to a watery death.

Gonzalo: These waves will take us, along with this ship that leaks.

Boatswain: Hold down the sails, men! Steer away from the wind.

Enter Mariners, wet

Mariners: We will all be carried to the bottom of the ocean by this disastrous storm!

Boatswain: What are you saying? If you believe that we are already doomed, there is no way for us to save ourselves.

Gonzalo: The king and prince are below praying that we will all find peace soon. We should go down and pray together with them.

Sebastian: I have no patience left for any of you.

Antonio: You are right; our worthy lives will be cut short by these reckless and unworthy mariners who have nothing to live for but the sea.

Gonzalo: I will not stop until I can ensure that my plans come together.

A confused noise within: "Mercy on us. Farewell, my wife and children. Farewell, brother!"

Antonio: We all should sink honorably and loyally with the king.

Sebastian: Not me! I say we abandon the king to his own watery grave.

Exit Antonio and Sebastian

Gonzalo: At this moment, I would give every drop of this boundless ocean for one small portion of parched land. However, should those above determine that I survive this night, I would wish for a dry death.

Element Focus: Setting

What kind of words does the boatswain
use to describe the storm?

#50982—Leveled Texts for Classic Fiction: Shakespeare

The Tempest

Act I, Scene I

◇◇◇

Sebastian: Kind mariner, where is the captain, the commander of this ship?

Boatswain: It would be preeminent for you to remain below; this is a frightening moment, and we are continuing to preserve this vessel from the storm.

Antonio: I will inquire again: Where is the captain who oversees this ship?

Boatswain: While you are above deck, you put yourself and the other men in danger. I tell you again: Go to your cabin below.

Gonzalo: No, no my good mariner; it is important that you hear me out.

Boatswain: The sea, with deep and strong waves, roars against us as if it were attempting to start a fight, and this water, weather, and wind does not care who you are. Now go to your cabin.

Gonzalo: Remember the significance and prominence of the personalities aboard.

Boatswain: Do you have an overwhelming power that makes you able to command the forces of nature? If so, demand that the darkening sky stop pummeling into us. If not, then find safety.

Exit

Gonzalo: When we make it securely through, I will see my plan to the finale.

Enter Boatswain

Boatswain: Pull down the top sail, and bring it together with the other sails!

A cry within

Oh, these cowardly men, who cry like babies, scream out their pitiful fear!

Enter Sebastian, Antonio, and Gonzalo

Not again; I ordered you to remain below, for is it your aspiration that we sink?

Sebastian: Who gives you the authority to communicate in such a method?

Boatswain: So be it, for if you desire to stay above deck, then you must work.

Antonio: Your rudeness toward us may get you in trouble, mariner. Besides, unlike you, we have no horror of being carried to a watery death.

Gonzalo: These waves will take us, along with this vessel that leaks.

Boatswain: Hold down the sails, men! Navigate away from the wind.

Enter Mariners, wet

Mariners: We will all be transported to the bottom of the ocean by this grievous storm!

Boatswain: What are you saying? If you believe that we are already doomed, there is no way for us to save ourselves.

Gonzalo: The king and prince are below praying that we will all find peace soon, and we should go down and pray together with them.

Sebastian: I have no tolerance left for any of you.

Antonio: You are precise; our worthy lives will be cut short by these reckless and unworthy mariners who have nothing to live for but the sea.

Gonzalo: I will not stop until I can ensure that my proposals come together.

A confused noise within: "Mercy on us. Farewell, my wife and children. Farewell, brother!"

Antonio: We all should sink honorably and loyally with the king.

Sebastian: Not me! I say we abandon the king to his own watery grave.

Exit Antonio and Sebastian

Gonzalo: At this moment, I would give every drop of this boundless ocean for one small portion of parched land. However, should those above determine that I survive this night, I would wish for a dry death.

Element Focus: Setting

What new element would you add to this setting to make it better?

Excerpt from

Henry V

Act IV, Scene III

Westmoreland: There is a hard battle ahead of us. I wish that we had a larger army. I wish that there were more Englishmen who would fight with us today.

King: No, do not wish for such a thing. If fate has said that we are to lose this battle, then we will. If we are to live, we will live. If we are to die, we will die. This battle will be hard for each of us. But if we do come out the winners, there is more honor in our fighting because there are so few of us. Do not wish that there were more men. The men here are kind and good men. I do not wish for more money in my life. I do not wish for more fine clothes. If I could wish for something, it would be to live and die as an honest man. No, no—do not wish for any more men. If there are any men among us who feel that this is not their battle, please let them leave. No person will think less of you. No man will speak against you. Men should fight for what they believe in. And if any of you here do not believe in our fight, you should be able to leave without harm. Some people celebrate this day in honor of a man named Crispin. Any man here today who comes home from this battle will also be celebrated. He will live through his life with this day always on his mind. His friends will honor him. His family will love him all the more for what he did on St. Crispin's Day. When he is old, he will tell his grandchildren of this day. He will tell them how he fought

for them. Time will go on. Years will pass. And that man may forget what he did here today. But the country will never forget. All people in England will know the names of the men who fight here today. It does not matter what part of the country you live in. Your actions here today will be remembered. And for the years to come, good men will teach their children how to be good men by telling them of Crispin's Day.

There may only be a few of us. But we are brothers. We are together in this battle. We will share the pain and glory. And the men who do not fight with us today will feel shame. They will wish they had been brave enough to be with us on St. Crispin's Day.

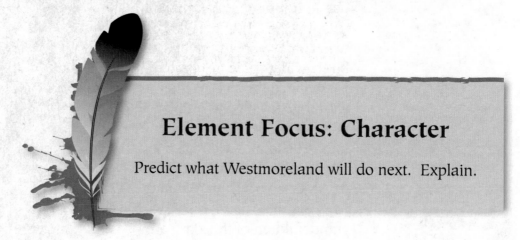

Element Focus: Character

Predict what Westmoreland will do next. Explain.

Excerpt from

Henry V

Act IV, Scene III

Westmoreland: There is a hard battle ahead of us. How I wish that we had a larger army. I wish that there were ten thousand more Englishmen who would come and fight with us today.

King: No, do not wish for such a thing. If fate has said that we are to lose this battle, then we will. If we are to live, we will live. If we are to die, we will die. This battle will be hard for each of us. But if we do come out the winners, there is more honor in our fighting because there are so few of us. Do not wish that there were more men. The men here are kind and good men. I do not wish for more money in my life. I do not wish for more fine clothes. But if I could wish for something, it would be to live and die as an honest and noble man. No, no—do not wish for any more men. In fact, if there are any men among us who feel that this is not their battle, please let them leave. No person will think less of you. No man will speak against you. Men should fight for what they believe in. And if any of you here do not believe in our fight, then you should be able to leave without harm. Some people celebrate this day in honor of a man named Crispin. Any man here today who comes home from this dangerous battle will also be celebrated. He will live through his life with this day always on his mind. His family and friends will honor him and love him all the more for what he did on St. Crispin's Day. Years from now, he will tell his

grandchildren of how he fought for them. Time will go on and that man may forget what he did here today. But the country will never forget. All people in England will know the names of the men who fight here today. It does not matter what part of the country you live in; your actions here today will be remembered. And for the years to come, good men will teach their children how to be good men by telling them of St. Crispin's Day.

There may only be a few of us. But we are brothers. We are together in this battle and will share the pain and glory. And the men who do not fight with us today will feel shame. They will hang their heads and wish they had been with us on St. Crispin's Day.

Element Focus: Character

What makes Westmoreland believable?

Excerpt from

Henry V

Act IV, Scene III

Westmoreland: There is a hard battle ahead of us, and I wish that we had a larger army. I wish that there were ten thousand more Englishmen who would come and fight with us today.

King: No, do not wish for such a thing. If fate has said that we are to lose this battle, then we will. If we are to live, we will live, and if we are to die, we will die. This battle will challenge each of us to be strong and fearless, but if we do come out the winners, there is more honor in our humble fighting because there are so few of us. Do not wish that there were more men. The men gathered for this fight are good and kind. I do not wish for more money in my life, nor do I wish for more fine clothes. But if I could wish for something, it would be to live and die with integrity. No, no—do not wish for any more men. In fact, if there are any men among us who do not believe in what we are fighting for, please do not hesitate to leave. No person here will think less of you. To fight rightly, men must fight for what they believe in, and if any of you here do not believe in our fight, then you should be able to leave. Some people celebrate this day in honor of a man named Crispin. Any man here today who comes home alive from this dangerous battle will also be celebrated. For years to come, he will remember and honor this day. His family and friends will praise him and love him all the more for the courage he showed on St. Crispin's Day. Years from now, he will tell his

grandchildren of how he fought for them. Time will go on and that man may forget the bravery he shows today. But, for centuries to come, all people in England will know the names of the men who fight here today. It does not matter what part of the country you live in; your actions here today will be remembered. And for the generations to come, good men will teach their children how to be good men by telling them of St. Crispin's Day.

There may only be a few of us, but we are brothers together in this battle, sharing the pain and glory. And the men who do not fight with us today will feel shame. They will hang their heads and wish they had been with us on Crispin's Day.

Element Focus: Character

What kind of leader is King Henry?

Excerpt from

Henry V

Act IV, Scene III

Westmoreland: There is a terrifying battle ahead of us today, and I wish that we had a larger army on our side. I wish that there were ten thousand more Englishmen who would rise up, and they would fight with us today.

King: No, do not wish for such a thing. If fate has determined we are to lose this battle, then that will be the outcome. If we are to live, we will live, and if we are to die, we will die. This battle will challenge the bravery and strength of each of us. But if, sadly, we do come out victorious, there is more honor in our humble fighting because there are so few of us against so many of them. Do not be fearful and wish that there were more men. The men here are honorable and trustworthy men. I do not wish for more money, nor do I wish for more fine clothes, but if I could wish for something to fulfill my life, it would be to live and die as an honest and noble man. No, no, do not wish for any more men. In fact, if there is any man among us who wavers in his belief in the rightness of this battle, please leave. No person here will think less of you, for some people celebrate this day in honor of a man named Crispin. Any man here today who comes home alive will also find this day celebrated in his honor. For years to come, he will remember all that he heroically faced on St. Crispin's Day, and he will live through his life with this day always on his mind. His family and friends will honor him and love him all the more for what he sacrificed on St. Crispin's Day. Years from now, he will tell his grandchildren of how he fought for them, and time will go on, and in his old age, that man may

forget what he boldly and daringly did here today. But, all the people in England will forever know the names of the men who fight here today. It does not matter what part of the country you live in; your actions here today will be remembered. And for the years to come, good men will teach their children how to be good men by telling them of St. Crispin's Day.

There may only be a few of us, but we are brothers, delighted to fight together in this battle, sharing the fear, the pain, the loss, and the glory. And the men from all over England who did not rise this morning to ride into this fight with us will feel shame tomorrow when they thank us for our work here today. Hanging their heads, they will wish they had been with us on Crispin's

Day.

Element Focus: Character

How does the speech reveal
the character of the king?

Excerpt from

Othello

Act I, Scene III

Othello: Her father loved me. He would ask me to come to his house. He wanted me to tell him stories about my life. He loved to hear me talk about the times I was in battle. He wanted to know about all the good times. He also wanted to know about all the hard times. I always told stories when he asked me to do so. I would talk about scary floods. I would talk about being hurt by other soldiers. I told about the many strange lands I had seen. During all of these stories, his daughter would sit and listen. Her name is Desdemona. Sometimes she would be called away to do her chores. But she would rush back to hear me talk. I knew that she wanted to hear more of my stories. I might tell a story of when I was hurt. She would say she was sorry for my pain. I might tell a story of

when I won a fight. She would be happy and laugh. She told me that she had always dreamed of her husband. He would be a brave man. He would be a strong man. I knew I wanted to marry Desdemona. So I used these stories to help her fall in love with me. I have done nothing else to her. I have retold the stories she loved to hear. If you do not believe me, ask her yourself. I see her coming now.

Duke of Venice: Well, those do sound like amazing stories. I know that my daughter would have loved to hear them, too. Brabantio, I think he is speaking the truth. Maybe she did want to be married to Othello. You think Othello forced her to marry him. But maybe you are wrong about that.

Brabantio: I want to hear what Desdemona has to say. If she says that she went with this man because she wanted to, then I will reject her. Come here, Desdemona. There are three men in this room. Which one of them is the most special to you?

Desdemona: My good father, I do not know how to answer that question. You are my father. I love you. I owe you for all you have done to raise me. I respect you. I want my actions to make you happy. But Othello is my husband. Now that I am married to him, things have changed. I must say that Othello is the most special.

Element Focus: Character

What are some possible explanations for Desdemona's decision?

#50982—Leveled Texts for Classic Fiction: Shakespeare

Othello

Act I, Scene III

Othello: Her father loved me. He would ask me to come to his house to tell him stories about my life. He loved to hear me talk about the times I was in battle. He wanted to know about all the wonderful times in my life as well as all the troubled times. And when he asked me to tell a story, I always did. I would talk about getting out of terrible floods. I would talk about being hurt and treated badly by other soldiers. I told about the deserts and forests and the strange lands I went to during my life. During all of these stories, his daughter, Desdemona, would sit and listen. Sometimes she would be called away to do her chores. But she would hurry back to be able to hear my stories. I knew that she wanted to hear more of my stories. She sighed and said she felt sorry for me if I told a story of when I was hurt. She was glad and happy when I told a story in which I won a battle. She told me that she had always dreamed that a man like me would come into her life. She knew that a brave and strong man was created just for her. I knew I wanted to marry Desdemona, and so I used these stories to help her fall in love with me. I have done nothing else to her. I have retold the stories she loved to hear. If you do not believe me, ask her yourself. I see her coming now.

Duke of Venice: Well, those do sound like amazing stories. I know that my daughter would have loved to hear them too. Brabantio, I think he is speaking the truth. Perhaps Desdemona did want to be married to Othello. Perhaps your idea that Othello forced Desdemona to marry him is not correct.

Brabantio: I want to hear what Desdemona has to say. If she says that she went with this man because she wanted to, then I will reject her. Come here, Desdemona. There are three men in this room. Which one of them is the most important to you?

Desdemona: My good father, I do not know how to answer that question. You are my father. I love you. I owe you for all you have done to raise me. I respect you and want my actions to make you happy. But Othello is my husband. Now that I am married to him, things have changed. I must say that Othello is the most important.

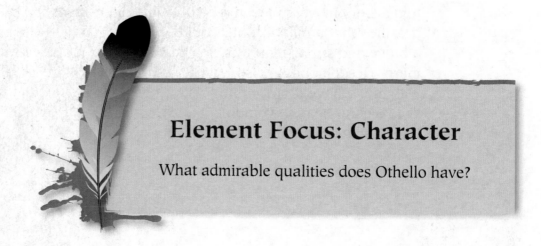

Element Focus: Character

What admirable qualities does Othello have?

#50982—Leveled Texts for Classic Fiction: Shakespeare

© Shell Education

Othello

Act I, Scene III

Othello: Her father loved me and he would ask me to come to his house to tell him stories about my life. He loved to hear me talk about the times I was in battle. He wanted to know about all of the wonderful times in my life as well as all the troubled times. And when he asked me to tell a story, I always did. I would talk about getting out of terrible floods or about being hurt and treated badly by other soldiers. I told about the dry deserts, rainy forests, and the many strange lands I went to during my life. During all of these stories, his daughter, Desdemona, would sit and listen. Sometimes she would be called away to do her chores, but she would hurry back to be able to hear my stories. I knew that she wanted to hear more of my stories because of how she acted. She sighed and

said she felt sorry for me if I told a story of when I was wounded or mistreated. She giggled and was happy when I told a story in which I won a victory. She told me that she had always dreamed that a man like me would come into her life. She knew that a brave and strong man was created just for her. And I knew I wanted to marry Desdemona, so I used these stories to help her fall in love with me. I have done nothing else to her but to tell her the stories she loved to hear. If you do not believe me, ask her yourself. I see her coming now.

Duke of Venice: Well, those do sound like amazing stories, and I know that my daughter would have loved to hear them, too. Brabantio, I think he is speaking the truth. Perhaps Desdemona did want to be married to Othello. Perhaps your idea that Othello forced Desdemona to marry him is not correct.

Brabantio: I want to hear what Desdemona has to say. If she says that she followed this man because it was her desire, then I will reject her. Come here, Desdemona. There are three men in this room. Which one of them is the most cherished in your heart?

Desdemona: My good father, I do not know how to answer that question. You are my father. I love you and I owe you for all you sacrificed to raise me. I respect you and your beliefs, and I want my actions to make you proud. But Othello is my husband and now that I am married to him, things have changed. My love and my heart belong to Othello; he is the most cherished person to me.

Element Focus: Character

What characteristics does Desdemona like about Othello? What does Brabantio think of Othello at the end of the passage?

Excerpt from

Othello

Act I, Scene III

Othello: Her father loved me, and he often would invite me to his house to tell him stories about my life, and he enjoyed my tales of battle and war. He wanted to know about all the wonderful times in my life, as well as all the troubled times. And when he asked me to tell a story, I always did. I would talk about escaping from floods and storms; about battles in which I was left bleeding and scarred; about being honored for bravery; or being mistreated. I told about the dry, brown deserts; rainy, damp forests; and the many exotic and strange lands that I visited. During all of these stories, his daughter, Desdemona, would sit and listen, and sometimes she would be called away to do her chores, and she would go quickly and hurry back to be able to hear my stories. I knew that she wanted to hear more of my stories because of how she acted. She sighed heavily, and she said she

felt sorry for me if I spoke about being wounded or abused. She giggled, clapped her hands together, and laughed when I told a story in which I was victorious, and she told me that she had always dreamed that a man like me would come into her life. That a man like me was surely just what the heavens had created for her. And I knew I wanted to marry Desdemona, for I knew that my stories were what she was attracted to in me, so I used these stories to help her fall in love with me. I have done nothing else to her but to tell her the stories she loved to hear, go ask her yourself. I see her coming now.

Duke of Venice: Well, those do sound like amazing and thrilling stories that I know my daughter would have wanted to hear, too. Brabantio, I think he is speaking the truth, and perhaps your idea that Othello forced Desdemona to marry him is not correct. It is possible that he did win her love, and he won her heart with his bravery and courage.

Brabantio: I want to hear what Desdemona has to say about this marriage, the one between herself and Othello. If she says that she followed this man into marriage, against my wishes, because it was her desire, then I will reject her. Come here, Desdemona, of the three men in this room, which one is the most beloved in your heart?

Desdemona: My good father, my heart is torn because I do not know how to answer that question. You are my father, and I love you and owe you for all you sacrificed to raise me. I respect you and your beliefs, and I want my actions to make you proud, but Othello is my husband, and now that I am married to him, things have changed. My heart belongs to Othello; he is the most important and beloved person to me.

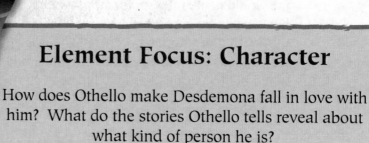

Element Focus: Character

How does Othello make Desdemona fall in love with him? What do the stories Othello tells reveal about what kind of person he is?

Excerpt from

RICHARD III

Act I, Scene I

Gloucester: Now finally all the sadness we have felt has passed. We are now finally at peace in this country after long wars. The world used to look dark and scary, but now that fear is far away. Our people feel joy because they have won the war. All of the pain we have gone through now seems worth it to them. But I do not feel that joy. The end of the war does not bring me peace. I am still deformed. My body is still ugly, and people do not look happily on me. I am so gross that even dogs bark in anger when they see me. And all of this hatred from people has not brought me peace. No. It has made me rude and mean inside. The country thinks we are done fighting, but I will keep the fighting going. I will lie and hurt those around me just to see them in pain. I have already done this to my own brother. King Edward loves my brother, and wants to see him have more power. But I have told the king of a dream. He thinks it is a real dream I had and that I speak truthfully, wanting to help him. But it is all a lie to make him turn against my brother. I have told the king that a man who has a *G* in his name will murder him. That will turn the king against my brother. Even though we call my brother Clarence, he is known throughout England as George. Here comes my brother now.

Enter Clarence, guarded, and Brakenbury

My good brother, what are you doing with this prison guard?

Clarence: The good king has sent this guard to take me to Tower Prison.

Gloucester: Good heavens! Why?

Clarence: Because my name is George.

Gloucester: But how is your name your fault? He should go after the parents or the grandparents. How can the king kill you for your name? Tell me how all of this happened.

Clarence: The king has heard from a man about a dream that told the future. The king believes this man. He thinks that his life is in danger. He believes that a man with a G in his name is going to murder him. And since George begins with a G, the king now believes I am that murderer. I have told him many times that I am not. But he is convinced, and there is no hope left for me.

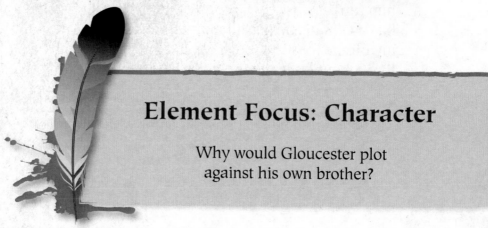

Element Focus: Character

Why would Gloucester plot
against his own brother?

#50982—*Leveled Texts for Classic Fiction: Shakespeare*

© *Shell Education*

RICHARD III

Act I, Scene I

◇◇

Gloucester: Now finally all the sadness we have felt has passed, and we are finally at peace in this country after long wars. The world used to look dark and scary, but now that fear has flown far away. Our people feel joy because they have won the war, and all of the pains of battle we have gone through seem worth it. But I do not feel that joy. The end of this bloody war does not bring me peace because I am still deformed. My body is still ugly, and people do not look happily on me. I am so gross that even dogs bark in anger when they see me. And all of this hatred from people has not brought me peace. No, it has made me cruel and nasty inside. The country thinks we are done fighting,

Edward' Rex quart'

but I will keep the fighting going. I will lie and hurt those around me just to see them feel some of the pain I have felt all my life. I have already done this to my own brother. King Edward loves my brother and wants to see him have more power. But I have told the king of a dream I had that told me the future. He thinks it is a real dream and that I speak truthfully, wanting to help him. But it is all a lie to make him turn against my brother. I have told the king that a man who has a G in his name will murder him. Even though we call my brother Clarence, he is known throughout England as George. Here comes my brother now.

Enter Clarence, guarded, and Brakenbury

My good brother, what are you doing with this prison guard?

Clarence: The good king has sent this guard to take me to Tower Prison.

Gloucester: Good heavens! Why?

Clarence: Because my name is George.

Gloucester: But how is your name your fault? If he wants to punish someone given the name of George, he should go after the parents or the grandparents. How can the king kill you for your name? Tell me how all of this happened.

Clarence: The king has heard from a man about a dream that told the future, and he believes this man and his dream. He thinks that his life is in danger and that a man with a G in his name is going to murder him. And since George begins with a G, the king now believes I am that murderer. I have told him many times that I would not hurt him. But he is convinced and there is no hope left for me.

Element Focus: Character

Why would Gloucester tell lies? What does that say about his character?

Excerpt from

RICHARD III

Act I, Scene I

Gloucester: Now finally all the sadness that our country has felt has passed and we have finally found a gentle peace after long wars. The world used to look dark and frightening, but now that fear has flown far away and left a shining light over the land. Our people feel delight once again because they have won the war, and the bitter pains of battle now seem worth it. But my heart does not beat with that joy because the swift end of this bloody war does not bring me peace. When I look at myself, I am still deformed, my body still ugly, and common people do not look at me. I am so disgusting to all creatures that even dogs bark in anger when they see me. And all of this hatred

Edward' kex quart'

from people has not brought me any contentment, but instead has also deformed me inside with horrible and offensive thoughts. The country thinks we are done fighting, but I will keep the fighting going. I will lie and hurt those around me just to see them feel some of the pain I have felt in my life. No one will be lucky enough to be spared because I have already done this to my own brother. King Edward loves my brother and wants to give him power, wealth, and land, but I have told the king of a dream I had that told me the future. He believes this is a real dream that unlocked secrets about the future to me. But, in truth, it is all a lie to turn him against my brother. I have told the king that my dream revealed that a man who has a G in his name will murder him. Even though we call my brother Clarence, he is known throughout England as George. Here comes my poor brother now.

Enter Clarence, guarded, and Brakenbury

My good brother, what are you doing with this guard?

Clarence: The good king has sent this guard to take me to Tower Prison.

Gloucester: Good heavens! Why would your good friend do such a thing?

Clarence: Because my name is George.

Gloucester: But how is your name your fault? If he wants to punish someone given the name of George, he should punish the parents or the grandparents. How can the king kill you for your name? Tell me how this terrible misunderstanding happened.

Clarence: The king has heard from a man about a dream that told the future and, trusting in this dream, the king has acted against me. He has been made to believe that his life is in danger and that a man with a G in his name is going to murder him. And since George begins with a G, the king now believes I am that murderer. I have told him many times that I would not hurt him, but he is convinced, and there is no hope left for me.

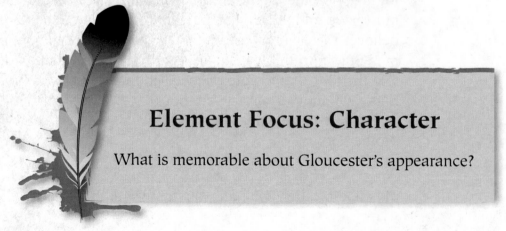

Element Focus: Character

What is memorable about Gloucester's appearance?

RICHARD III

Act I, Scene I

Gloucester: Now finally all the sorrow that our country has felt has passed, and we have finally found a gentle peace after long and vicious wars. The world used to look shadowy and frightening, but now that fear has flown far away and left a shining light over the land. Our people feel delight once again because they have won the war, and the bitter pains of battle seem worth it. But my heart does not beat with their delight because the swift end of this bloody war does not bring me peace. When I look at myself, I am still deformed, my body still ugly, and common people do not look at me; their joy does not mean they will accept the ugliness of my appearance. I am so disgusting to all creatures that even dogs bark in anger when they see me. And all of this hatred from people has not

Edward rex quart

brought me any contentment, but instead has also deformed me inside with hideous and belligerent thoughts. The country believes the war is over, but I will keep the fighting going with the rage I feel against my fellow men. I will lie, cheat, and destroy those around me just to see them feel some of the agonizing pain I have felt every day of my life. No one will be fortunate enough to be spared from the offensive plans of my heart because I have already betrayed my own brother. King Edward loves my brother and wants to award him power, wealth, and property, but I have told the king of a dream I had that revealed the future to me. King Edward believes this is a real dream that unlocked secrets about the future to me, but in truth, it is all a lie created to turn him against my brother. I have explained to the king that my dream indicated that he will be murdered by a man who has a G in his name. Even though we call my brother Clarence, he is known throughout England as George. Here comes my poor brother now.

Enter Clarence, guarded, and Brakenbury

My good brother, what are you doing with this guard?

Clarence: The good king has sent this guard to take me to Tower Prison.

Gloucester: Good heavens! Why would your good friend do such a thing?

Clarence: He says it is because my name is George.

Gloucester: But how is your name your fault? If he wants to punish someone given the name of George, he should punish the parents or the grandparents since they determined the name. How can the king kill you for your name? Tell me how this terrible injustice happened.

Clarence: The king has heard from a man about a dream that told the future and, trusting in this dream, the king has acted against me. He has been made to believe that his life is in danger and that a man with a G in his name is going to murder him. And since George begins with a G, the king now believes I am that murderer. I have told him many times that I would not hurt him as we are good friends who have known each other since childhood, but he is convinced, and there is no hope left for me.

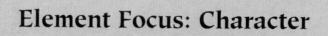

Element Focus: Character

What is Gloucester's motivation for behaving cruelly? How does he justify his cruelty?

Excerpt from

The Winter's Tale

Act II, Scene II

Paulina: Kind sir, will you find the man in charge of this prison for me? Let him know that I am here. I have come to see the queen.

Exit gentleman

How can such an honest woman like the queen be in such a horrible jail? All the people of Europe look at her as good and pure. What could she have done to be in jail by her husband?

Enter gentleman with the guard

My good man. You are a guard here in this jail. You watch over our queen. You know who I am, don't you?

Guard: A fine and lovely lady whom it is an honor to know.

Paulina: Please do me a favor then. Take me to the queen.

Guard: I am not allowed to do that. The king has ordered that no one may go to visit her.

Paulina: This is nonsense. How could he lock up his own wife? And she is such a wonderful and generous woman. And worse, to keep her friends from her? Has he also taken her ladies from her? Has he ordered that she suffer all alone? What about her best friend, Emilia?

Guard: He has wanted the queen to be all alone. But Emilia has refused to leave. To help you feel better, I will ask Emilia to come out so that you can speak with her.

Paulina: Yes, please. Let me speak with Emilia. Will all of you please leave us so that we may talk alone?

Exit gentleman and attendants

Guard: Everyone else can feel free to leave. But I must stay and hear what you have to say.

Paulina: If it must be that way, then it must be that way.

Guard returns with Emilia

Oh, Emilia, how is the queen doing?

Emilia: As happy as one can be who is jailed by her husband. To make things worse, in all of the sadness and confusion, she has had her baby early.

Paulina: A boy?

Emilia: No. A beautiful baby girl. The baby is strong and seems to want to live. All good things since she came so early. The queen already loves her so much. She speaks to her and holds her close. She is so sad that her child must be born in such a gross and dirty place. And her sadness is made worse because both the queen and the young baby are innocent.

Paulina: I cannot believe this king has done such a cruel thing. How dare he! He had better watch out for me. He must know that his own sweet baby girl has been born in the dirt of a jail. Tell the queen that I have a plan to help her get out. I will take the baby to the king. When he sees her, he will understand that she is his child. He will see his love for her. He will remember how much he loves his queen.

Emilia: What a wonderful plan. And how brave and generous of you to want to fight for our queen and her child. It has been a great mistake to put our queen in here. But you will make it all right again. I will tell the queen of this plan. We must do all we can to bring the king and queen together. Her heart would be broken if he rejected her again.

Paulina: Go tell her of our plan, Emilia. I will do all that I can to make this right again.

Element Focus: Character

What does the queen do that
shows she is a good mother?

The Winter's Tale

Act II, Scene II

◇◇

Paulina: Kind sir, will you find the man in charge of this prison for me and let him know that I am here? I have come to see the queen.

Exit gentleman

How can such a gentle and innocent woman like the queen be in such a horrible jail? How can that be when all the people of Europe look at her as pure and kind? What could she have done to be sent to jail by her husband?

Enter gentleman with the guard

My good man, you are a guard here in this jail and you watch over our queen. You know who I am, don't you?

Guard: A fine and lovely lady whom it is an honor to know.

Paulina: If you believe I work for good, please do me a favor. Take me to the queen.

Guard: I am sorry, but I am not allowed to do that. The king has ordered that no one may go to visit her.

Paulina: This is nonsense. How could he lock up his own wife, who everyone knows is a wonderful and generous woman? And worse, to keep her friends from her? Has he also taken her ladies from her? Has he ordered that she suffer all alone? What about her best friend, Emilia?

Guard: He has wanted the queen to be all alone, but Emilia has refused to leave. I want to help you, and the best I can do is to ask Emilia to come out so that you can speak with her.

Paulina: Yes, please, let me speak with Emilia. Will all of you please leave us so that we may talk alone?

Exit gentleman and attendants

Guard: Everyone else can feel free to leave, but I must stay and hear what you have to say.

Paulina: If it must be that way, then it must be that way.

Guard returns with Emilia

Oh, Emilia, how is the gentle queen doing?

Emilia: She does her best to be at peace, but she is only as happy as one can be who is jailed by her husband. And to make things worse, in all of the sadness and confusion, she has had her baby early.

Paulina: A boy?

Emilia: No, a beautiful daughter. The baby is strong, and even though she is little, she seems to want to live. The good queen already loves her so much. She speaks softly to her and holds her close, trying to forget that her child is in such a gross and dirty place. And her sadness is made worse because the queen and the young baby are innocent.

Paulina: I cannot believe this king has done such a cruel thing. How dare he! He had better watch out for me. He must know that his own sweet baby girl has been born in the dirt of a jail. Tell the queen that I have a plan to help her get out. I will take the new baby to the king. When he sees her, he will understand that she is his child. He will remember how much he loves his queen.

Emilia: What a wonderful plan. And how brave and generous of you to want to fight for our queen and her child. It has been a great mistake to put our queen in here. But you will make it all right again. I will tell the queen of this plan. We must do all we can to bring the king and queen together. Her heart would be broken if he rejected her again.

Paulina: Go tell her of our plan, Emilia. I will do all that I can to make this right again.

Element Focus: Character

How does the guard know he can trust Paulina?
What do most people think of the queen?

#50982—*Leveled Texts for Classic Fiction: Shakespeare*

© *Shell Education*

Excerpt from

The Winter's Tale

Act II, Scene II

Paulina: Kind sir, will you locate the man in charge of this prison for me and let him know that I am here to see the queen?

Exit gentleman

I do not understand how such a kind-hearted, gentle, and innocent woman like the queen could be imprisoned. Certainly there must be some great error as everyone knows her to be pure and honorable. What offensive misconduct could she have committed?

Enter gentleman with the guard

My good man, you are a guard here in this jail, and you oversee our queen. You know who I am, don't you?

Guard: Yes, a fine and lovely lady whom it is an honor to know because you live your life to do what is factual and just.

Paulina: Please do me a favor and take me to the queen.

Guard: I am sorry, but I am not permitted, by order of the king, to allow any companions to see the queen.

Paulina: This is nonsense. On what authority does the king think he can imprison his own wife, whom everyone knows is a thoughtful and generous woman? Now he also commands that her friends must be kept away? Has he taken her ladies from her? Has he ordered that she agonize all alone? What about her best friend, Emilia?

Guard: The king did order that the queen be jailed alone, but her faithful friend, Emilia, has refused to leave her side. The best offer I can make to help calm your heart is to call for Emilia and have her report to you on how the queen is handling herself in jail.

Paulina: Yes, please, let me communicate with Emilia. Will all of you please leave us so that we may talk in isolation?

Exit gentleman and attendants

Guard: Everyone else can feel free to leave, but on the orders of the king, I must stay and hear what you have to say.

Paulina: If it must be that way, then it must be that way.

Guard returns with Emilia

Oh, Emilia, how is the gentle queen doing?

Emilia: She does her best to be at peace, but she is only as happy as one can be who is jailed by her husband. And to make things worse, in all of the sadness, confusion, and desperation, her baby has come early.

Paulina: What has she had? A boy?

Emilia: No, a beautiful and strong daughter. Despite being born premature, the baby has fight in her. The good queen already adores her so much. She spends her time speaking softly to the child, holding her close, and trying to soothe away the pain of being here in this jail.

Paulina: I am amazed and in disbelief that the king has done such a cruel thing. How dare he! He had better watch out for me because of the mean-spirited words I have for him. He must know that his own precious infant daughter has been born in the grimy dirt of this prison. Tell the queen that I have devised a plan. I will take the baby to the king, and when he sees the face of his child, he will understand his mistake. The deep love he will feel for his own child will melt his heart; he will know again how affectionately he loves his wife.

Emilia: What a magnificent plan; and how wonderfully courageous of you to want to fight for our queen and her child. It has been a great mistake to imprison our kind queen and an even greater mistake in allowing the princess to be born here. I will tell the queen of this plan. We will do all we can to bring the king and queen together again because her wounded heart would be forever fragmented if rejected.

Paulina: Go tell her of our plan. I will do what is within my power to make this right.

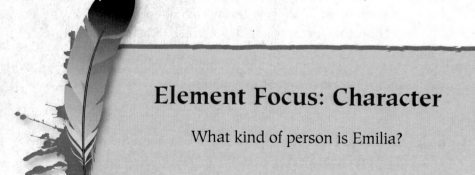

Element Focus: Character

What kind of person is Emilia?

#50982—Leveled Texts for Classic Fiction: Shakespeare

The Winter's Tale

Act II, Scene II

◇◇

Paulina: Kind sir, will you locate the man in charge of this prison for me, and let him know that I am here to see the queen?

Exit gentleman

I do not comprehend how such a kind-hearted, gentle, and innocent woman like the queen could be imprisoned. Certainly there must be some great inaccuracy as everyone knows her to be wholesome and honorable. What offensive misconduct could she have committed?

Enter gentleman with the guard

My good man, you are a guard here in this jail, and you oversee our queen. You know who I am, don't you?

Guard: Yes, a fine and lovely lady whom it is an honor to know because you live your life to do what is factual and just.

Paulina: Please do me a favor, and please take me to the queen.

Guard: I am sorry, but I am not permitted. By order of the king, he has requested to not allow any companions to see the queen.

Paulina: This is nonsense, on what authority does the king think he can imprison his own wife, whom everyone knows is a thoughtful and generous woman? Now he also facilitates that her friends must be kept away? Has he taken her ladies from her? Has he ordered that she agonize all alone? What about her best friend, Emilia?

Guard: The king did order that the queen be jailed alone, but her faithful friend, Emilia, has refused to leave her side. The best offer I can make to help calm your heart is to call for Emilia, and ask her to report to you on how the queen is handling herself in jail.

Paulina: Yes, please, let me communicate with Emilia. Will all of you please evacuate, so that we may talk in isolation?

Exit gentleman and attendants

Guard: Everyone else can feel free to leave, but on the orders of the king, I must stay, and I must hear what you have to say.

Paulina: If it must be that way, then it must be that way.

Guard returns with Emilia

Oh, Emilia, how is the gentle queen doing?

Emilia: She does her best to be at peace, but she is only as happy as one can be who is jailed by her husband, and to make things worse, in all of the sadness, confusion, and desperation, her baby has come prematurely.

Paulina: What has she had? A boy?

Emilia: No, a beautiful and strong daughter. Despite being born premature, the baby has fight in her. The good queen already adores her so much, and she spends her time speaking softly to the child, holding her close, and trying to soothe away the discomfort of being here in this jail.

Paulina: I am amazed and in disbelief that the king has done such a cruel thing. How dare he! He had better watch out for me because of the mean-spirited words I have for him. He must know that his own precious infant daughter has been born in the grimy dirt of this prison. Tell the queen that I have devised a scheme, for I will take the baby to the king and when he sees the face of his child, he will understand his mistake. The deep love he will feel for his own child will melt his heart, and he will know again how affectionately he loves his wife.

Emilia: What a magnificent plan, and how wonderfully courageous of you to want to battle for our queen and her child. It has been a great mistake to imprison our kind queen and an even greater mistake in allowing the princess to be born here. I will tell the queen of this plan, and we will do all we can to bring the king and queen together again because her wounded heart would be forever fragmented if rejected.

Paulina: Go tell her of our plan. I will do what is within my power to make this right.

Element Focus: Character

What words does Paulina use to characterize the king and his actions? What words does she use to characterize the queen?

Excerpt from

Hamlet

Act IV, Scene VII

King Claudius: There should be no place in the world that allows murder. But revenge is different. Revenge is not murder. It should have no rules. It is paying someone back for doing something wrong to you. And if you want revenge on Hamlet for killing your father, I have a plan. Come close and listen to what I am thinking. Hamlet knows you have just come back from school. I will praise you in front of him. I will tell him of all of the wonderful things you learned while in school. I will make Hamlet jealous of you. Then I will suggest that you and Hamlet have a fight with swords. I will say that it will be to show off all of the skills you have learned. I will make it known that no one will be hurt in this pretend fight. But you and I will know better. We will put poison on the tip of your sword. You will not have to hurt Hamlet in any way. All you will have to do is prick the sword's tip against his arm. In this way, you may have revenge for your father.

Laertes: I will do it. While I was at school, I found some very strong poison. It is so dangerous that just a drop of it will kill a man. I will dip the tip of my sword in that poison.

King Claudius: But we have to make sure that this plan will not fail. So I have something else we can do, too. At the start of the fight, I will pour a cup of wine for Hamlet. I will toast him so he will think I support him. Then I will put a pearl into the wine. Everyone will think I am doing it to honor Hamlet. But we will know that the pearl has already been dipped into the poison. Then when Hamlet is hot and out of breath from your fight, he will drink from the cup. And that will ensure that he does not make it out alive.

Enter Queen Gertrude

My lovely Queen! What is the matter?

Queen Gertrude: One sad event just seems to lead to another sad event. Laertes, your sister is drowned. Ophelia is drowned.

Laertes: Drowned! Where? How?

Queen Gertrude: There is a beautiful tree that grows near a small creek. She sat down by the creek and began to make herself a crown of flowers. It was so pretty with all the colors and softness of the flowers. But then she went to the side of the creek. She wanted to see her reflection in the glassy water. But she lost her balance. And into the water she tumbled. The water carried her for a while. She floated like a mermaid. The flowers around her head made her seem like an angel. She sang children's songs, unaware of the danger she was in. But soon her clothes became heavy because of the water. Her thin body began to sink into the water. But she did not seem to notice or care. She kept singing until the water had covered her. In the silence, she found her death.

Laertes: How can that be?

Queen Gertrude: She is drowned.

Laertes: Your death came because of too much water, Ophelia. So I will not cry watery tears. But I will make sure to get revenge for your death— your death and the death of our father.

Element Focus: Plot

How does Ophelia's death affect Laertes's plan?

Hamlet

Act IV, Scene VII

King Claudius: There should be no place in the world that allows murder, but revenge is different. Revenge is not murder, and it should have no rules because it is hurting someone who hurt you. And if you want revenge on Hamlet for killing your father, I have a plan. Come close and listen to what I am thinking. Hamlet knows you have just returned home from school. I will praise you in front of him. I will tell him of all the wonderful things you learned while in school and make Hamlet jealous of you. Then I will suggest that you and Hamlet have a fight with swords. I will say that it will be to show off all the skills you have learned while you were away at school. I will make it known that no one will be hurt in this pretend fight, but you and I will know better. We will put poison on the tip of your sword so you will not have to hurt Hamlet in any way. All you will have to do is prick the sword's tip against his arm. You will look innocent to all the palace. In this way, you may have revenge for your father.

Laertes: I will do it. While I was at school, I found some very strong poison. It is so dangerous that just a drop of it will kill a man. I will dip the tip of my sword in that poison.

King Claudius: But we have to make sure that this plan will not fail, so I have something else we can do, too. At the start of the fight, I will pour a cup of wine for Hamlet. I will toast in honor of Hamlet to show my support for him. Then I will put a pearl into the wine. Everyone in the palace will think I am doing it to honor Hamlet, but we will know that the pearl has already been dipped into the poison. Then when Hamlet is tired and out of breath from your fight, he will drink from the cup, and that will ensure that he does not make it out alive.

Enter Queen Gertrude

My lovely queen! What is the matter?

Queen Gertrude: One sad event just seems to lead to another sad event. Laertes, your sister is drowned. Ophelia is drowned.

Laertes: Drowned! Where? How?

Queen Gertrude: There is a beautiful tree that grows near a small creek. She sat down by the creek and began to make herself a crown of flowers. It was so pretty with all the colors and softness of the flowers. Then she went to the side of the creek because she wanted to see her reflection in the glassy water. But when she leaned over the water, she lost her balance and tumbled into the water. The water carried her for a while, and she floated like a mermaid. The flowers around her head made her seem like an angel, and she sang children's songs, unaware of the danger she was in. But soon her clothes became heavy because of the water, and her thin body began to sink. She did not seem to notice or care, but kept singing until the water had covered her. In the silence, she found her death.

Laertes: How can that be?

Queen Gertrude: She is drowned.

Laertes: Your death came because of too much water, Ophelia, so I will not cry watery tears. But I will make sure to get revenge for your death— your death and the death of our father.

Element Focus: Plot

What is the likelihood that Claudius and Laertes will follow through with their plan? Explain.

Excerpt from

Hamlet

Act IV, Scene VII

King Claudius: There should be no place in the world that allows murder, but revenge is not murder. It is different and should have no rules. If you want revenge on Hamlet for killing your father, come close and listen, because I have a plan. Hamlet knows you have just returned home from school. I will praise you in front of him and tell him of all of the wonderful things you learned while in school. This will make Hamlet jealous of you, which is just what we want. Playing on this jealousy, I will suggest that you and Hamlet have a fight with swords and I will say that it will be to showcase the skills you learned while you were away at school. I will make it known to everyone that no one will be hurt in this pretend fight, but you and I will know better. We will put poison on the tip of your sword so you will not have to hurt Hamlet. All you will have to do is prick the sword's tip against his arm. You will look innocent of Hamlet's sudden death to everyone in the palace. In this way, you may have revenge for your father.

Laertes: I will do it. I have the perfect poison. While I was at school, I found some strong poison. It is so dangerous that just a drop of it will kill a man very quickly. I will dip the tip of my sword in that poison and use it during my duel with Hamlet.

King Claudius: But we have to make sure that this plan will not fail so I have something else we can do, too. At the start of the fight, I will pour a cup of wine for Hamlet, toast to show my support for Hamlet to the people, and then drop a pearl into the cup. Everyone in the palace will think I am doing it to honor Hamlet, but we will know that the pearl has already been dipped into the poison. Then when Hamlet is tired and out of breath from your fight, he will drink from the cup, and that will ensure that he does not make it out alive.

Enter Queen Gertrude

My lovely queen! What is the matter?

Queen Gertrude: One sorrowful event seems to bring about another sorrowful event. Laertes, your sister, Ophelia, is drowned.

Laertes: Drowned! Where? How?

Queen Gertrude: There is a beautiful tree that grows near a small creek. She sat down by the creek and began to make herself a crown of soft and beautiful flowers. Once she had dressed herself with her creations of flowers, she went to the side of the creek to see her reflection in the glassy water. But when she leaned over the water, she lost her balance and tumbled into the water. The water carried her for a while and she floated like a mermaid with her clothes spread out around her. The crown of flowers made her seem like an angel as she sang children's songs, unaware of the danger she was in. But soon her clothes became heavy as they drank the water, and her thin body began to sink under the weight. She did not seem to notice or care, but kept singing until the water had covered her. In the silent water, she found her death.

Laertes: How can that be?

Queen Gertrude: She is drowned.

Laertes: Your death already has too much water, beautiful Ophelia, so I will not cry watery tears in my sadness, but instead I will make sure to get revenge for your death— your death and the death of our father.

Element Focus: Plot

What is odd about Ophelia's death? Why would Laertes seek revenge against Hamlet?

Excerpt from

Hamlet

Act IV, Scene VII

King Claudius: There should be no place in the world that allows murder, but revenge is not murder; revenge is different and should have no rules and no boundaries. If you want revenge on Hamlet for killing your father, come close and listen, because I have a plan. Hamlet knows you have just returned home from school. I will praise you in front of him, and I will tell him of all of the wonderful things you learned while in school. This will make Hamlet jealous of you. Playing on this jealousy, I will suggest that you and Hamlet have a fight with swords, and I will say that it will be to showcase the skills you learned while you were away at school, and Hamlet will agree so that he can lessen his own feelings of guilt. I will make it known to everyone that no one will be hurt in this pretend fight, but secretly, you and I will know the true intention of the duel: Hamlet's death. We will put poison on the tip of your sword so you will not have to hurt Hamlet outwardly. All you will have to do is prick the sword's tip against his arm, and you will look innocent of Hamlet's sudden and unexpected death to everyone in the palace, and you will have your revenge for your father.

Laertes: I will do it, for I have the perfect poison already. While I was at school, I found some very strong poison that is so dangerous that just a drop of it will kill a man very quickly. It is this poison that will sharpen the tip of my sword during my duel with Hamlet.

King Claudius: But we have to ensure that this plan does not fail, so I have another way we can guarantee Hamlet's death. At the start of the fight, I will pour a cup of wine for Hamlet, toast to show my support for Hamlet to the people, and then drop a pearl into the cup. Everyone in the palace will think I am doing it to honor Hamlet, but we will know that the pearl has already been dipped into the poison. Then when Hamlet is tired and out of breath, he will drink from the cup, and that will ensure that he does not make it out alive.

Enter Queen Gertrude

My lovely queen! What is the matter?

Queen Gertrude: One sorrowful event seems to bring about another sorrowful event. Laertes, your sister, Ophelia, is drowned.

Laertes: Drowned! Where? How?

Queen Gertrude: There is a beautiful willow tree that grows near a small creek. Ophelia sat down by the creek and began to make herself a crown of soft and beautiful flowers. Once she had dressed herself with her flowery creations, she went to the side of the creek to see her reflection in the glassy water. But when she leaned over, she lost her balance and tumbled into the water, and the water carried her for a while and she floated like a mermaid, her clothes spread out. The crown of flowers made her appear like an angel as she sang children's songs, unaware of the danger. But soon her clothes became heavy as they drank the water, and her thin body began to sink under the pressure. She did not seem to notice, but kept singing until the water covered her; in the silent water, she found her death.

Laertes: How can that be?

Queen Gertrude: She is drowned.

Laertes: Your death already has too much water, beautiful Ophelia, so I will not cry watery tears in my sadness, but instead I will take revenge for your premature death—your death and the death of our father.

Element Focus: Plot

What might be Claudius's motive for keeping his plan against Hamlet secret from everyone but Laertes? How does Claudius plan to manipulate Hamlet into agreeing to the sword fight?

Excerpt from

King Lear

Act I, Scene I

King Lear: And now we can talk about the reason we are all gathered together. Hand me that map. This is a map of my kingdom. You can see here that I have drawn lines to divide the land into three parts. I am an old man. I have ruled my kingdom for many years. Now it is time for me to stop working so hard. It is time for my daughters to take care of the kingdom. They are young and strong and can make sure the kingdom is taken care of. I have a plan to choose who will get the most power. Each daughter will come and tell me and all the people of the palace how much she loves me. The daughter who can convince me that her love is the strongest will get the largest piece of land and the most power. Goneril is the oldest of my children. You may come forward and speak first.

Goneril: Father, I love you more than I can tell you. There are not enough words in the world to tell you how deep and rich my love is for you.

Cordelia: [Aside] What can I say when it is my turn? I love him with more honesty than my selfish sisters. But they will say anything to get power. I shall love him as I always have. But I will not play this game of lies.

King Lear: That is a wonderful answer, Goneril. I will give you this rich piece of land. It has deep forests, meadows for planting, and rivers of delicious water. And now, Regan, you are my second child. You may come forward and tell me how much you love me.

Regan: Father, I love you with just as much passion as Goneril. I want nothing but to make you happy. Your approval is all that I want in the world. I would turn away anyone who does not work for your pleasure.

Cordelia: [Aside] My sisters are cruel liars. They say this only to get the land and money from our father.

King Lear: And I will be your happy father knowing you love me this much. To you, I will give this other piece of land. It has just as much richness and beauty as the piece I gave to Goneril. Now Cordelia. My third child. My most favorite daughter. Come and tell me how much you love me.

Cordelia: I have nothing to say, Father.

King Lear: Nothing?

Cordelia: Nothing.

King Lear: If you say nothing, you will get nothing. Think carefully. Then speak of your love for me.

Cordelia: I wish that my heart could speak, but it cannot. And I will not speak fake words of love to my own father.

King Lear: Stop and think, Cordelia. If you do not say what I want to hear, you are putting your future in danger.

Cordelia: You are my father. You are a wonderful father. You created me. You brought me up with love. For all that, I honor and respect you. I have lived my life trying to obey and be the daughter you wanted me to be. But I will not lie to you. My sisters speak to you with false words. They tell you that they love you more than any other person, but both of them are married. The words they speak for you are against their own husbands. I love you, Father, but I will not lie to you.

Element Focus: Plot

What is King Lear doing with the land that makes up the kingdom? What does he want each of his daughters to tell him?

Excerpt from

King Lear

Act I, Scene I

King Lear: And now we can talk about the reason we are all gathered together. Hand me that map of our kingdom. You can see here that I have drawn lines to divide the land into three parts. I am an old man who has ruled this kingdom for many years. Now it is time for me to stop working so hard and for my daughters to take care of the kingdom. They are young and strong and can make sure the kingdom is taken care of for the future. I have a plan to choose who will get the most power. Each daughter will come and tell me and all the people of the palace how much she loves me, and the daughter who can convince me that her love is the strongest will get the largest piece of land and the most power. Goneril is the oldest of my children. You may come forward and speak first.

Goneril: Father, I love you more than I can tell you. There are not enough words in the world to tell you how deep and rich my love is for you.

Cordelia: [Aside] What can I say when it is my turn? I love him with more honesty than my selfish sisters do, but they will say anything to get power. I shall love him as I always have. But I will not play this game of lies.

King Lear: That is a wonderful answer, Goneril. I will give you this rich piece of land. It has deep forests, meadows for planting, and rivers of delicious water. And now, Regan, my second child, come forward and tell me how much you love me.

Regan: Father, I love you with just as much passion as Goneril. I want nothing but to make you happy. Your approval is all that I want in the world. I would turn away anyone who does not work for your pleasure.

Cordelia: [Aside] My sisters are cruel liars. They say this only to get the land and money from our father.

King Lear: And I will be your happy father knowing you love me this much. To you I will give this other piece of land that has just as much richness and beauty as the piece I gave to Goneril. Now Cordelia, my third and favorite daughter, come and tell me how much you love me.

Cordelia: I have nothing to say, Father.

King Lear: Nothing?

Cordelia: Nothing.

King Lear: If you say nothing, you will get nothing. Think carefully, and then speak of your love for me.

Cordelia: I wish that my heart could speak, but it cannot, and I will not speak fake words of love to my own father.

King Lear: Stop and think, Cordelia. If you do not say what I want to hear, you are putting your future in danger.

Cordelia: You are my father, and you are a wonderful father. You created me; you brought me up with love. For all that, I honor and respect you. I have lived my life trying to obey and be the daughter you wanted me to be, but I will not lie to you. My sisters speak to you with false words. They tell you that they love you more than any other person, but both of them are married. The words they speak for you are against their own husbands. I love you, Father, but I will not lie to you.

Element Focus: Plot

What problems does King Lear create in dividing his kingdom?

#50982—*Leveled Texts for Classic Fiction: Shakespeare*

Excerpt from

King Lear

Act I, Scene I

King Lear: And now we can speak about the reason we are all gathered together. Hand me that map of our kingdom. You can see here that I have drawn lines to divide the land into three parts. I am an old man who has ruled this kingdom for many years. The time has come for me to stop working so hard and to pass onto my three lovely daughters the responsibilities of this kingdom. They are young, strong, and smart and will ensure that the kingdom remains healthy and lasts long into the future. I have great power to hand over today, and to ensure that the right daughter wins that power, I have a plan. The daughter who pleases me the most will earn the biggest reward. Each daughter will come and tell me and all the people of the palace how much she loves me, and the daughter who can convince me that her love is the greatest will get the largest piece of land and the biggest share of the power. Now, Goneril, the oldest of my daughters, come forward and speak.

Goneril: Father, I love you more than I can tell you. There are no words powerful enough in the wide world to express how deep and rich my love is for you.

Cordelia: [Aside] What can I say when it is my turn? I love him with more honesty than my selfish sisters, but they will say anything to get the power he is handing out. I shall love him as I always have in my heart, but I will not play this game of lies.

King Lear: That is a wonderful answer, Goneril, and for it I will give you this rich piece of land. It has deep forests for hunting, vast meadows for planting, and rushing rivers of delicious water. Now, Regan, my second daughter, come forward and tell me how much you love me.

Regan: Father, I love you with just as much passion as Goneril. I want nothing but to make you happy. Your approval is all that I want in the world. I would turn away anyone who does not work for your pleasure.

Cordelia: [Aside] My sisters are cruel liars. They say this only to grab the land and money our father is foolishly giving away.

King Lear: And I will be your happy father knowing you love me this much. To you, I will give this other piece of land that has just as much richness and beauty as the piece I gave to Goneril. Now Cordelia, my third, my youngest, my most favorite daughter, come and tell me how much you love me.

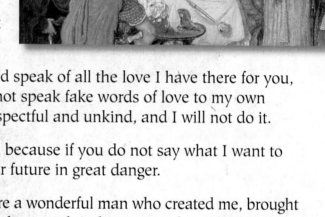

Cordelia: I have nothing to say, Father.

King Lear: Nothing?

Cordelia: Nothing.

King Lear: If you say nothing, you will get nothing. Think carefully, and then speak of your love for me.

Cordelia: I wish that my heart could speak of all the love I have there for you, but it cannot, and I will not speak fake words of love to my own father. It would be disrespectful and unkind, and I will not do it.

King Lear: Stop and think, Cordelia, because if you do not say what I want to hear, you are putting your future in great danger.

Cordelia: You are my father. You are a wonderful man who created me, brought me up, loved me, and taught me to be what I am today. Throughout my life, I have tried to obey you, but I will not lie to you. Not for your benefit or for my own. My sisters speak lies to you so that they can take your power, wealth, and fortune, but I do not want those things. My sisters speak false words that say they love you more than any other person, both of them are married, and their love must go to their husbands. The words they speak for you are against their own husbands. I love you father, but I will not lie to you.

Element Focus: Plot

Why does Cordelia refuse to tell her father what he wants to hear? What reasons does Cordelia give to prove that Goneril and Regan are lying?

Excerpt from

King Lear

Act I, Scene I

King Lear: And now we can speak about the reason we are all gathered together. Hand me that map of our kingdom. You can see here that I have drawn lines to divide the land into three parts, each part containing the abundance of our land. I am an old man who has ruled this kingdom well for many years, but I have decided it is time for me to stop working every day and ask my lovely daughters to share the responsibility of ruling our vast kingdom. My daughters are intelligent, strong-willed, and determined young women who will ensure that the affairs of the kingdom are handled with care and justice. But there is much power and wealth in this position, so I have created a test that they must pass. Each of my daughters will come forward and tell me and all the people of the palace how much she loves me, and the daughter who can convince me that her love is the strongest will receive the largest piece of land and the greatest share of the power. Now, Goneril, my oldest daughter, come forward and speak.

Goneril: Father, I love you more than I can express in words. There are not enough words of affection in the wide world to tell you how deep and rich my love is for you.

Cordelia: [Aside] What can I say when it is my turn? I love him with more honesty than my selfish sisters, but they will say anything to get power, and he will believe them. I shall love him as I always have in my heart, but I will not play this game of lies.

King Lear: That is a wonderful answer, Goneril, and for it, I will give you this rich piece of land. It has deep forests for hunting, vast and rolling meadows for planting and harvesting, and rushing rivers of delicious water. Now, Regan, my second daughter, come forward.

Regan: Father, I love you with just as much passion as Goneril. I want nothing but to make you happy and to earn your approval in the actions I take. I would turn away anyone who does not work for your pleasure.

Cordelia: [Aside] My sisters are cruel liars. They say this only to snatch the land and money from our foolish father.

King Lear: And I will be your happy father knowing you love me this much. To you, I will give this other piece of land that has just as much richness and beauty as the piece I gave to Goneril. Now Cordelia, my third daughter, my youngest child, my most favorite daughter, come forward and tell me how much you love me.

Cordelia: I have nothing to say, Father.

King Lear: Nothing?

Cordelia: Nothing.

King Lear: If you say nothing, you will get nothing. Think carefully, and then speak of your love for me.

Cordelia: I wish that my heart could speak what it feels, but it cannot, and I will not speak fake words of love to my own father just because he wants to hear them.

King Lear: Stop and think before you speak again Cordelia because if you fail to speak the words I want to hear, you are putting your future in danger.

Cordelia: You are my father, a wonderful man who created me, raised and nurtured me, loved me, and taught me to be what I am today. Throughout my life, I have tried to obey you and be the daughter you wanted me to be, and that daughter respects and honors you too much to lie to you. I cannot and I will not speak falsely to you for your benefit and certainly not for my own. My sisters speak lies to you so that they can steal your power, wealth, and fortune. My sisters speak false words that say they love you more than any other person but both of them are married, and their love must go to their husbands. How can they love you with everything they have when they have husbands to whom they have given their hearts? The words they speak for you are against their own husbands. I love you, Father, and I am sad that I have disappointed you, but I will not lie to you.

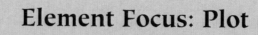

Element Focus: Plot

How does Cordelia's response prove that she loves her father more than her sisters?

Excerpt from

Macbeth

Act I, Scene VII

Macbeth: If I am going to kill the king, I must do it fast. I cannot stop to think about what I am doing. If I kill him, I will get to be king, and that is what I want. I cannot think about King Duncan because I must think about getting what I want. I cannot let myself imagine what might happen if others find out what I have done. King Duncan is here in my house. He trusts me to treat him well. I have no reason not to treat him well. He is a kind friend. He is a wise king. Part of me feels such guilt for what I am about to do to him. But there is another part of me that wants the power he has. Which part of me will win this battle?

Enter Lady Macbeth

My wife. What is the news of King Duncan?

Lady Macbeth: He is almost done eating his dinner. I thought we agreed that you would hide in his room.

Macbeth: Has King Duncan asked where I am?

Lady Macbeth: Why would he do that?

Macbeth: I do not want to do this anymore. Duncan is a generous king. He has just given me a new and more important job. If I am going to be king, I think I should just wait for it to happen on its own.

Lady Macbeth: How can you say that? Last night, we both agreed that you would take Duncan's life. You wanted to be king. You have such hope in yourself. Have you become afraid? Are you willing to live your life never having the courage to take what you want?

Macbeth: Stop this. I have acted always with bravery. Any man who acts selfishly for himself and not for what is right is not a real man.

Lady Macbeth: So last night when we planned this, you were not a man? We spoke to each other about how you wanted to be king. You want to be king. I helped you make a plan to get you what you want. Last night, you did not seem to mind what that plan meant for King Duncan. How can he matter now? If I were you, I would be able to do what we planned.

Macbeth: But what if our plan fails?

Lady Macbeth: How can we fail? We have made a plan. As long as we see the plan through, we will not fail.

Element Focus: Plot

Why do Macbeth and Lady Macbeth make a plan to kill the king?

Excerpt from

Macbeth

Act I, Scene VII

Macbeth: If I am going to kill the king, I must do it fast. I cannot stop to think about what I am doing and let myself feel guilty about my actions. If I kill him, I will get to be king, and that is what I want. I must imagine how great I will feel when I am king and not about the horrible thing I must do to become king. I cannot let myself think about what might happen if others find out about what I have done. King Duncan is here in my house, and he trusts me to treat him well. I have no reason not to treat him well. He is a kind friend, a wise king, and he has always treated me with respect. Part of me feels such guilt for what I am about to do to him, but another part of me wants the power he has. Which part of me will win this battle?

Enter Lady Macbeth

My wife, what is the news of King Duncan?

Lady Macbeth: He is almost done eating his dinner. I thought we agreed that you would hide in his room.

Macbeth: Has King Duncan asked where I am?

Lady Macbeth: Why would he do that?

Macbeth: I do not want to do this anymore. Duncan is a generous king and has just given me a new and more important job in the kingdom. If I am going to be king, I think I should just wait for it to happen on its own.

Lady Macbeth: How can you say that? Last night, we both agreed that you would take Duncan's life. You wanted to be king, and you believed that now was the time to act to get the power and wealth you always thought was yours. You had such hope in yourself when we made our plan. Have you become afraid? Are you willing to live your life never having the courage to take what you want?

Macbeth: Stop this. I have acted always with bravery in every battle I have fought. Any man who acts selfishly for himself and not for what is right is not a real man.

Lady Macbeth: So last night when we planned this, you were not a man? We spoke to each other of our dreams for the future. You want to be king, and together we created a plan to get you what you want. Last night, you did not seem to mind what that plan meant for King Duncan. How can he matter now? If I were you, I would be able to do what we planned. I would not be a coward and worry with guilt.

Macbeth: But what if our plan fails?

Lady Macbeth: How can we fail? We have made a plan, and as long as we see the plan through, we will not fail.

Element Focus: Plot

Why does Macbeth feel guilty about wanting to murder King Duncan?

Excerpt from

Macbeth

Act I, Scene VII

Macbeth: If I am going to kill the king, I must do it fast and without any thought. I cannot allow myself to stop and think about what I am doing or allow myself to feel guilt about my actions. If I kill him, I will become king and that is what I want. I must imagine how great I will feel when I am king and not about the horrible thing I must do to become king. I cannot permit my thoughts to create guilt and sorrow in me. How can I imagine taking violent action against him when I have no reason at all to feel negatively toward him? He is a loyal friend, a wise and just king, and he has always treated me with respect. Even this week, he has given me a great honor, and I would repay his trust by taking his life so that I can have power. Part of me feels such extreme guilt for what I am considering doing to him, but another part of me craves the power he has and wants to do whatever is needed to have it. Which part of me will win this battle?

Enter Lady Macbeth

My wife, what is the news of King Duncan?

Lady Macbeth: He is almost done eating his dinner, and I thought we agreed that you would hide in his room.

Macbeth: Has King Duncan asked where I am?

Lady Macbeth: Why would he do that?

Macbeth: I do not want to do this anymore. Duncan is a noble and worthy king who does not deserve the cruelty we are planning against him. If I am going to be king, I think I should just wait for the title to come to me in its own time.

Lady Macbeth: How can you say that? Last night, we both agreed that you would take Duncan's life. You have a desire and a need to be king, and when we talked last night, you believed that now was the time to act. Yesterday, there was no worrying and feeling guilt and you knew what you had to do to grasp the power and wealth you have always known was yours. You had such hope in yourself when we made our plan. Have you become afraid? Are you willing to live your entire life never having the courage to take what you want?

Macbeth: Stop this mean-spirited speech. I have acted always with bravery and integrity in every battle I have fought. Any man who takes an angry and selfish action for himself and not for what is right is not a real man.

Lady Macbeth: So last night when we planned this, you were not a man? We spoke to each other of our dreams for the future and you told me you knew it was your destiny to be king, and together we created a plan to make that dream true. Last night you did not seem to mind what that plan meant for King Duncan. How can he matter now? If I were you, I would be able to do what we planned. I would not be a coward and worry with guilt.

Macbeth: But what if our plan fails?

Lady Macbeth: How can we fail? We have made a plan, and as long as we see the plan through, we will not fail.

Element Focus: Plot

What makes Macbeth change his mind about the plan?

Macbeth

Act I, Scene VII

Macbeth: If I am going to murder the king, I resolve to act quickly. I cannot allow myself to pause or to think about what I am doing, because then I will only feel guilt about my actions. If I kill him, I will become king, and being king is what I want. Instead of considering the horrific acts I must commit to become king, I must focus on how great I will feel when I finally am king. King Duncan is here as a guest in my house, and as a guest, he should be treated with honor and generosity. He is a loyal friend, a wise and just king, a strong and responsible commander, and he has always treated me with respect. Even this week, he has bestowed a great honor on me, and I would repay his trust in me by taking his life for no other reason than to steal his power. Part of me feels such extreme guilt for contemplating the murder of my king. But another part of me craves the power he has and will do whatever is necessary to have it. Which part of me will win this battle?

Enter Lady Macbeth

My wife, what is the news of King Duncan?

Lady Macbeth: He is almost done eating his dinner, but why are you here when we agreed that you would hide in his room?

Macbeth: Has King Duncan asked where I am?

Lady Macbeth: Why would he do that?

Macbeth: I do not want to do this anymore. Duncan is a noble and worthy king, he does not deserve the cruelty we are planning. If I am meant to be king, I should simply wait for the title to come to me in its own time.

Lady Macbeth: How can you say that, my husband, when we both decided last night that you would take Duncan's life? You had such unshakable hope in yourself when we devised our plan and believed in the signs that indicated that now, this moment, is the time to act. Have you become afraid and fearful of your desire to be king? Are you willing to live your entire life never having the courage to take what you want?

Macbeth: Stop this mean-spirited speech. I have acted always with bravery and integrity in every battle I have fought, for any man who takes a wicked and selfish action for himself and not for what is right is not a real man.

Lady Macbeth: So last night when we planned this, you were not a man? We spoke to each other of our dreams for the future, and you told me you knew it was your destiny to be king. So together, we created a plan to make that dream true. Last night, you did not seem to mind what that meant for King Duncan, and how can he matter now when we are so close to getting what we want? If I were you, I would be able to do what we planned, and I would be willing to sacrifice anything to get you what you wanted, even if that meant throwing my own child away.

Macbeth: But what if our plan fails?

Lady Macbeth: How can we fail? We have made a plan, and as long as we see the plan through without giving into fear, we will not fail.

Element Focus: Plot

How does Lady Macbeth convince Macbeth to follow through on their plan to murder King Duncan? Predict the outcome of the plan.

Excerpt from

Much Ado About Nothing

Act II, Scene III

Don Pedro: Come here. We are playing a trick on Benedick. We want him to think that Beatrice is in love with him. I will now speak loudly so he can hear us. So you think that Beatrice is in love with Benedick?

Claudio: Benedick is sitting where he can hear you. Keep talking. Yes, I think she is. I have never seen a lady so in love with a man.

Leonato: Me either. It is good that she loves him. But it is also odd. She always acts as if she hates him.

Benedick: Is it possible? Does Beatrice care for me?

Leonato: I think that her love for him is very strong. Then, she feels as if she cannot say her love, so her feelings come out as anger.

Don Pedro: Maybe she is just acting. Her anger may be pretend.

Claudio: Maybe you are right. Her anger toward Benedick is just pretend.

Leonato: So every time she acts as if she hates Benedick, she is acting. So, what she really feels is love? The mean words are really loving words?

Don Pedro: What kinds of things has she done to make you think she loves Benedick?

Claudio: Benedick is listening to us. He believes what we are saying. Keep going. Our plan is working well.

Leonato: My daughter tells me about the things Beatrice does. Beatrice does many things that show her secret love for Benedick.

Claudio: Yes, I have heard about some things, too.

Don Pedro: This is amazing. Beatrice acts as if she hates being around men.

Leonato: And I would think that her hatred is strongest against Benedick. Just look at the way she acts around him. But I guess that her anger is at herself. She cannot tell him how she feels in her heart.

Benedick: I am amazed at what I am hearing. But my heart feels happiness about Beatrice.

Claudio: Benedick believes what we are saying. Keep going.

Don Pedro: Has she told Benedick how she feels?

Leonato: No. She has promised herself that she never will tell him.

Claudio: Yes, Beatrice is in a fight with her heart. She does not think she can tell Benedick that she loves him. She is afraid he will not believe her. Why would he? She has always been so mean to him.

Leonato: My daughter tells me that sometimes Beatrice stays up all night. She tries to write letters to Benedick. But then she rips the letters in two pieces. Beatrice says that she knows that Benedick would laugh and say hurtful things to her if he knew her true feelings.

Claudio: Sometimes Beatrice falls onto her knees. She cries for the love she feels for Benedick.

Leonato: Yes, my daughter has told me of that as well. My daughter thinks Beatrice will do something crazy because she loves Benedick.

Don Pedro: I think that someone should tell Benedick. It would help put poor Beatrice out of pain.

Claudio: Benedick would tease Beatrice and use this information to hurt her.

Don Pedro: And that would be terrible. Beatrice is a lovely lady.

Claudio: And she is very, very smart.

Don Pedro: She is very smart in many ways, but not in loving Benedick.

Element Focus: Plot

Why do the men say that it is strange that Beatrice is in love with Benedick? How do the men think Benedick will behave when he learns of Beatrice's love for him?

Much Ado About Nothing

Act II, Scene III

Don Pedro: Come here, Leonato. We are playing a trick on Benedick. We are going to talk loudly so he can overhear. We want him to believe that Beatrice is in love with him. I will now speak loudly enough for him to overhear us. Leonato, do you think Beatrice is in love with Benedick?

Claudio: Benedick is sitting just where he can hear you. Keep talking. Yes, I have never seen a lady so in love with a man.

Leonato: Me either. It is wonderful that she loves Benedick. But it is strange since she always acts as if she hates him.

Benedick: Is it possible that Beatrice does care for me?

Leonato: I think that her love for him is so strong that when she feels it, she does not know what to do. Instead, her feelings come out as anger.

Don Pedro: Maybe she is pretending to not like him.

Claudio: Maybe you are right. Her anger toward Benedick may be pretend.

Leonato: So every time she acts as if she hates Benedick, she is pretending? What she really feels is a great love for him? So when she says mean words against Benedick, she really means loving words?

Don Pedro: What things has she done to make you think she loves Benedick?

Claudio: Benedick is listening and he believes what we are saying. Keep going. Our plan is working well.

Leonato: My daughter told you of some of the things Beatrice does to show her secret love for Benedick.

Claudio: Yes, she did.

Don Pedro: This is amazing. Beatrice always acts as if she cannot stand to be around most men.

Leonato: Certainly, I would think that her hatred is strongest against Benedick. But I guess that her anger is at herself for not telling him how she feels in her heart.

Benedick: I am amazed at what I am hearing. But my heart feels happiness about Beatrice.

Claudio: Benedick believes what we are saying. Keep going.

Don Pedro: Has she told Benedick how she feels?

Leonato: No, and she has promised herself that she never will tell him.

Claudio: Yes, your daughter has told me about Beatrice's fight with her heart. Beatrice does not think she can tell Benedick that she loves him since she has been so mean to him.

Leonato: My daughter tells me that sometimes Beatrice stays up all night trying to write letters to Benedick. But then she rips the letters in two pieces. Beatrice says that she knows that Benedick would laugh and say hurtful things to her if he knew her true feelings.

Claudio: I hear Beatrice falls on her knees and cries for all the love she feels for Benedick.

Leonato: Yes, my daughter has told me of that as well. My daughter thinks that Beatrice will do something crazy because she loves Benedick.

Don Pedro: I think that someone should tell Benedick. It would help put poor Beatrice out of pain.

Claudio: Benedick would tease Beatrice and use this information to hurt her.

Don Pedro: That would be terrible. Especially since Beatrice is a lovely lady.

Claudio: And she is very, very smart.

Don Pedro: She is very smart in many ways, but not in loving Benedick.

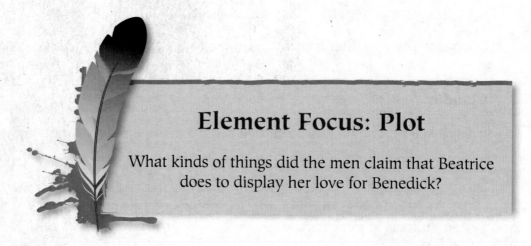

Element Focus: Plot

What kinds of things did the men claim that Beatrice does to display her love for Benedick?

Excerpt from

Much Ado About Nothing

Act II, Scene III

Don Pedro: Come here, Leonato. We are playing a trick on Benedick, and we are going to talk loudly so he can overhear what we say. We want him to believe that Beatrice is in love with him, so I will now speak loudly. Leonato, do you think Beatrice is in love with Benedick?

Claudio: Benedick is sitting just where he can hear you, so keep talking. Yes, I have never seen a lady so in love with a man.

Leonato: Me either, and it is wonderful that she loves Benedick, but it is also strange, since she always acts as if she hates him.

Benedick: Is it possible that Beatrice does care for me?

Leonato: I think that her love for him is so strong that when she feels it, she does not know what to do. Her feelings come out as anger.

Don Pedro: Maybe she is pretending to not like him.

Claudio: Maybe you are right that her anger toward Benedick is just pretend.

Leonato: Every time she acts as if she hates Benedick, she is acting, but her true feelings are love? You think that when she says mean words against Benedick, what she really means are loving words?

Don Pedro: What kinds of things has she done to make you believe that she loves Benedick?

Claudio: Keep going because Benedick is listening and he believes what we are saying. Our plan is working well.

Leonato: My daughter told you some of the things Beatrice does to show her secret love for Benedick.

Claudio: Yes, she did share those things. Can you tell about them?

Don Pedro: This is amazing to think about, since Beatrice always acts as if she cannot stand to be around most men.

Leonato: But certainly, based on her actions, I would think that her hatred is strongest against Benedick, but I guess that her anger is at herself for not being able to tell him how she feels in her heart.

Benedick: I am amazed at what I am hearing, but my heart feels such joy thinking that Beatrice loves me.

Claudio: Benedick believes what we are saying, keep going.

Don Pedro: Has she told Benedick how she feels?

Leonato: No, and she has promised herself that she never will tell him.

Claudio: Yes, your daughter has told me about how Beatrice fights with her heart. For so long, Beatrice has teased and spoken to Benedick with harsh words, that now she is sure he would never believe that she loves him.

Leonato: My daughter tells me that sometimes Beatrice stays up all night trying to write letters to Benedick that express her love for him. But she always ends up tearing the letters in two. Beatrice is convinced that if Benedick were to know her feelings, he would make fun of her.

Claudio: Your daughter has talked about how Beatrice falls on her knees and cries for all the love she feels for Benedick.

Leonato: Yes, my daughter has told me of that as well. My daughter worries that Beatrice might do something crazy because she loves Benedick.

Don Pedro: If Beatrice will not tell him, I think that someone should tell Benedick. It would help put poor Beatrice out of the pain she is in.

Claudio: Why should anyone tell him? Benedick would only tease her, speak cruelly to her, and use this information to hurt her.

Don Pedro: And that would be terrible, given what a lovely lady Beatrice is.

Claudio: Yes, and on top of all that, she is very intelligent.

Don Pedro: She is very smart, but not when it comes to loving Benedick.

Element Focus: Plot

Predict what Benedick will do next, now that he believes that Beatrice loves him.

#50982—*Leveled Texts for Classic Fiction: Shakespeare*

Excerpt from

Much Ado About Nothing

Act II, Scene III

Don Pedro: Leonato, come and help us with a trick we are playing on Benedick. We are going to speak loudly, so he can overhear our conversation. We are going to make him believe that Beatrice loves him, so I will now speak loudly. Do you really think Beatrice is in love with Benedick?

Claudio: Benedick is sitting just where he can hear you; keep talking. Yes, I have never seen a lady so madly in love with a man.

Leonato: Me either. It is so wonderful that she loves Benedick, but it is also so strange because she always acts as if she hates him.

Benedick: Is it possible that Beatrice does care for me?

Leonato: I think that her love for him confuses her. Instead of being able to express how much she loves him, her feelings come out as feelings of anger.

Don Pedro: Maybe it is all an act, and she is only pretending to not like him.

Claudio: Maybe you are right that her anger is just a pretend mask to hide her feelings.

Leonato: So you are saying that every time she acts mean outwardly, she is pretending and inwardly she feels a passionate love for him? And when they meet, her cruel words are really just hiding her love?

Don Pedro: What kinds of things has she done to convince you that she loves Benedick when all her actions convey a dislike for him?

Claudio: Keep going, for our plan is working well. Benedick is listening to all we say, and he believes what we are saying about Beatrice.

Leonato: My daughter told you of some of the things Beatrice does when she is alone that prove her secret love for Benedick.

Claudio: Yes, she did. Will you explain some of those things to us?

Don Pedro: This is amazing to hear, because Beatrice normally acts as if she cannot stand to be around most men.

Leonato: Given her words and actions, it seems that her hatred is strongest against Benedick; however, after hearing this, I think that her anger is at herself for not telling Benedick how she feels in her heart.

Benedick: I am amazed at what I am hearing, but there is great joy in my heart to think that Beatrice loves me.

Claudio: I can tell that Benedick believes what we are saying, so keep talking.

Don Pedro: Has she told Benedick how she feels?

Leonato: No, and she has promised herself that she never will tell him.

Claudio: Yes, your daughter has told me that Beatrice is in a bitter battle with her heart, and she wants to tell Benedick how much she loves him, but she does not believe that he would treat her with respect.

Leonato: My daughter tells me that sometimes Beatrice stays up all night trying to write love letters to Benedick, but that she always ends up ripping the letters into two pieces. She is convinced that if she reveals her love to Benedick, he will make fun of her and refuse to believe her.

Claudio: And your daughter has told me of how Beatrice falls on her knees and cries for all the love she feels for Benedick.

Leonato: Yes, my daughter has told me of that as well, and my daughter worries that Beatrice may do something crazy because she loves Benedick.

Don Pedro: If Beatrice will not tell him on her own, I think that someone else should, which would help put poor Beatrice out of pain.

Claudio: Why should anyone tell him? Benedick would tease Beatrice, make her feel insignificant and silly, and use this information to hurt her.

Don Pedro: It would be terrible for Beatrice, who is such a generous lady.

Claudio: And beyond that, she is extremely intelligent.

Don Pedro: She is very intelligent in most of her life, but not in loving Benedick.

Element Focus: Plot

How do you know the trick is working on Benedick?

Excerpt from

The Merchant of Venice

Act V, Scene I

Lorenzo: The moon is shining so brightly tonight. The breeze seems to kiss the leaves of the trees. This kind of night makes me think of the fairy tales I was told as a child. I think of all the men and women who loved each other in those stories. But they were always kept apart by something unfair. Like the story of Troilus. He loved a wonderful lady named Cressida. They could not be together because of a violent war.

Jessica: Yes, my love. Clear nights like this make me think of those stories as well. Like the story of Thisbe. She was to meet the man she loved, Pyramus. But in the silent night, she heard a lion. And in her fear, she ran away. And the two were never able to be together.

Lorenzo: It is on a night like this that so many love stories have happened. Nights when women stood waiting for their men to return to them.

Jessica: On a night like tonight, women make promises to love. Then they take actions to prove the power of their love. Sometimes, those women must betray their families for the love of a man.

Lorenzo: Yes, just as you have done on this night. My poor Jessica, you have had to lie to your father. You have left the safety of your home. You have come out into the dark woods. And all just to be with me.

Jessica: And on this clear night, my love, Lorenzo, you promised me your love.

Lorenzo: And on this night, my Jessica, you did not believe me. But I proved my love to you. And we now look with happiness toward our life together.

Jessica: And what a happy night tonight is for us. But I hear someone coming.

Enter Stephano

Lorenzo: Who is there?

Stephano: Do not worry. I am a friend.

Lorenzo: A friend to us? What friend are you? What is your name?

Stephano: My name is Stephano. I have come here from my lady. She wants to help you and Jessica be together. But you must come with me now so that she can get you both ready to be married.

Lorenzo: Is there anyone else there with her?

Stephano: She has only her maid with her.

Lorenzo: Come on, Jessica, let us go with this man. He will take us to where we can be married.

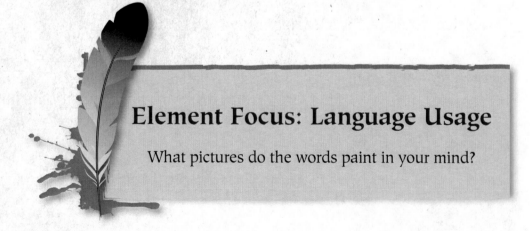

Element Focus: Language Usage

What pictures do the words paint in your mind?

Excerpt from

The Merchant of Venice

Act V, Scene I

Lorenzo: The moon is shining so brightly tonight. The breeze seems to come and kiss the leaves of the trees. This kind of night makes me remember all the fairy tales I was told as a child. It makes me think of all the men and women who loved each other, but were kept apart by something unfair. Like the story of Troilus, who loved the beautiful lady Cressida. They could not be together because of a violent and ugly war.

Jessica: Yes, my love. Beautiful and clear nights like this remind me of lovers who are forced to be apart from each other. Like the story of Thisbe. She was to meet the man she loved, Pyramus. But in the silent night, she heard a lion coming toward her. And in fear for her own life, she ran away.

Lorenzo: It is on a night like this that so many love stories have happened. So many women have waited for their men to return to them.

Jessica: Or it is a night that women make promises and take actions that prove their love. Those women must betray their fathers or their families for the love of a man.

Lorenzo: Yes, just as you, my love, my Jessica, have done on this night. My poor love, you have had to disrespect your father. You had to leave the safety of your home to come far out to the woods. And all to be with me.

Jessica: And on such clear nights as this, my love, Lorenzo, you promised me your love.

Lorenzo: And on this night, my Jessica, you did not believe me. But I proved my love to you, and we now look with happiness toward our life together.

Jessica: And what a happy night tonight is for us. But I hear someone coming.

Enter Stephano

Lorenzo: Who is there?

Stephano: Do not worry. I am a friend.

Lorenzo: A friend to us? What friend are you? What is your name?

Stephano: My name is Stephano. I have come here from my lady. She wants to help you and Jessica be together. But you must come with me now so that she can get you both ready to be married.

Lorenzo: Is there anyone else there with her?

Stephano: She is there alone except for her maid.

Lorenzo: Come on, Jessica, let us go with this man. If he will take us to where we can be married, we should follow him.

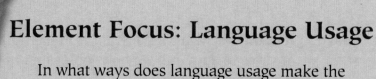

Element Focus: Language Usage

In what ways does language usage make the description of the location vivid?

Excerpt from

The Merchant of Venice

Act V, Scene I

Lorenzo: The moon is shining so brightly tonight, and the breeze seems to come and kiss the leaves of the trees. This kind of night makes me remember all the fairy tales I was told as a child. It makes me think of all the sad stories of men and women who loved each other but were always kept apart by something unfair. Like the story of Troilus and his beautiful love, Cressida. They could not be together because of a violent and brutal war.

Jessica: Yes, my love, beautiful and clear nights like this remind me of the stories of lovers who are forced to be apart from each other. Like the story of Thisbe, who was to meet the man she loved, Pyramus, in the woods. From there, they were to leave to begin a new life together, but in the silent night, she heard a lion coming toward her. Fearing for her life, she ran away.

Lorenzo: It is on a night like this that so many love stories have happened. In these stories, women stood patiently waiting for their men to return to them.

Jessica: Or it is on a night like tonight that women make promises and then take actions that prove the power of their love. On those nights, women must betray their fathers or families for the love of a man.

Lorenzo: Yes, just as you, my love, my Jessica, have done on this night. My poor love, you have had to disrespect your father, leave the security of your home, and come far out into the dark woods. And all to be with me.

Jessica: And on such clear nights as this, my love, Lorenzo, you promised your love just like in those fairy tales.

Lorenzo: And on this night, my Jessica, you did not believe me when I told you of my love. But I proved my love to you and, after forgiving you for not believing me, we look with happiness toward our future life together.

Jessica: And what a happy night tonight is for us because we can finally get the fairy tale ending that we want. Wait, I hear someone coming through the trees.

Enter Stephano

Lorenzo: Who is there?

Stephano: Do not worry. I am a friend to you.

Lorenzo: A friend to us? What friend are you? What is your name?

Stephano: My name is Stephano. I have come here from my lady who wants to help you and Jessica be together. You must come with me now to my lady so that she can prepare you both for your marriage to each other.

Lorenzo: Is there anyone else there with her?

Stephano: She is there alone except for her maid.

Lorenzo: Come on, Jessica, let us go with this man. If he will take us to where we can be safely married, we should follow him.

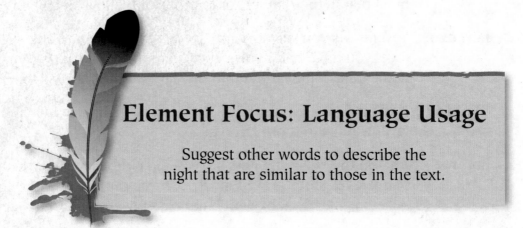

Element Focus: Language Usage

Suggest other words to describe the night that are similar to those in the text.

Excerpt from

The Merchant of Venice

Act V, Scene I

Lorenzo: The moon is shining so brightly tonight, and the breeze seems to come from the heavens and kiss the leaves of the trees. This kind of gentle night makes me remember all the fairy tales I was told as a child, all of the tragic stories of men and women who loved each other passionately, but were inevitably kept apart by something unfair. Like the story of Troilus and his beautiful love, Cressida, who could not be together because a violent and brutal war tore them apart.

Jessica: Yes, my love, crystal-clear nights like this remind me of the stories of lovers who are forced to be separate from each other. Like the story of Thisbe, who was to meet the man she loved, Pyramus, in the woods. In the silent night, she heard a lion stalking toward her, and fearing for her life, she ran away.

Lorenzo: It is on a night like this that so many love stories have happened, stories where women have patiently waited for their men to return to them.

Jessica: Or it is on a night like tonight that women make promises, declare their love, and then take actions that betray their fathers, their friends, and their families to prove the power of that love.

Lorenzo: Yes, just as you, my love, my Jessica, have done on this night. My poor Jessica, you have been made to disrespect your father, leave the safety and security of your home, and travel in the darkness into the frightening woods, to be with me.

Jessica: And on such clear nights as this, my love, Lorenzo, you promised me your love for all eternity, just like in those fairy tales.

Lorenzo: And on this night, my Jessica, you did not believe me when I told you of my love, but once I proved my love to you and forgave you for not believing, we look with happiness toward our future life together.

Jessica: And what a happy night tonight is for us because we can finally get the fairy tale ending that we want. Wait, I hear someone coming through the trees.

Enter Stephano

Lorenzo: Who is there?

Stephano: Do not worry. I am a friend to you.

Lorenzo: A friend to us? What friend are you? What is your name?

Stephano: My name is Stephano. I have come here from my lady who wants to help you and Jessica be together. You must come with me now to my lady so that she can prepare you both for your marriage to each other.

Lorenzo: Is there anyone else there with her?

Stephano: She is there alone except for her maid.

Lorenzo: Come on, Jessica; let us go with this man because if he can take us to where we can be safely married, we should follow him.

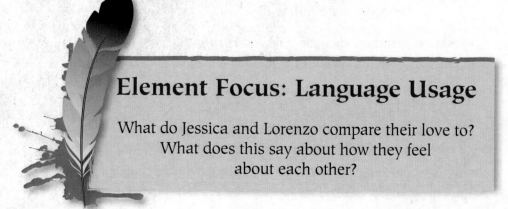

Element Focus: Language Usage

What do Jessica and Lorenzo compare their love to? What does this say about how they feel about each other?

Excerpt from

A Midsummer Night's Dream

Act II, Scene I

Titania: Please calm down. This child that you want to take from me is not mine. Her mother was a good friend of mine. We used to sit together in the cool night air and talk. We loved to sit on the beach to smell the salt air and watch the waves. We would watch as the ships came into the harbor. They were always loaded with treasures. She would compare herself to the ships'

sails. They would grow round and fat when filled with the wind. She said it was just like her round and fat belly that held her baby. Often, she would go into the town. She would bring me back something special from the ships. But she was not a fairy like we are. No, she was human. And like all humans, she could die. When her baby was born into the world, she died and was taken away. But she was such a wonderful friend to me. So I promised to raise her child. And because I made such a promise, I will not allow you to have the child.

Oberon: How long are you planning to stay in these woods?

Titania: Maybe until after Theseus's wedding. If you will be kind and patient, come and be with us. If you feel you must act rudely, please leave. I will stay away from your favorite places. That way, we do not have to see each other.

Oberon: Give me that boy. Then I will happily stay with you.

Titania: There is no way you can have this child. Come all my fairies, we must leave. Oberon and I will have a terrible fight if we stay here.

Exit Titania with her fairies

Oberon: That is fine, Titania. But be warned. I will punish you for not giving me what I want. My servant, Puck, come here. Do you remember the time we sat on that island? It was out in the ocean. And how that mermaid was singing? And how she rode on the back of that dolphin?

Puck: I remember.

Oberon: While you were listening to her song, I saw something. Up in the sky, Cupid was flying. He had with him his bow and arrow. As you watched the mermaid, he shot an arrow down into a meadow on the island. I watched the arrow as it flew. And I saw where it landed. In the meadow, there was a white flower that young ladies liked to stop and smell. But when that flower was hit with Cupid's arrow, it turned purple. It was as if the flower had been bruised by the arrow. Go and get that flower for me. The juice of that flower has a special power. When it is put on the eyelids of someone sleeping, it will make the sleeper fall in love with the first live creature he or she sees after waking up. Hurry and go get that flower for me.

Puck: I will be there and back in no time at all.

Exit

Oberon: Once I have this flower, I will use it on Titania. I will put the juice of the flower on her eyes. I will make her fall in love with something horrible, maybe a bear or an ape or a lion. And because she has the juice in her eyes, she will love this monster with her whole heart. Then, I will be able to get that child from her. Wait, I hear someone coming. I will become invisible and hear what they have to say.

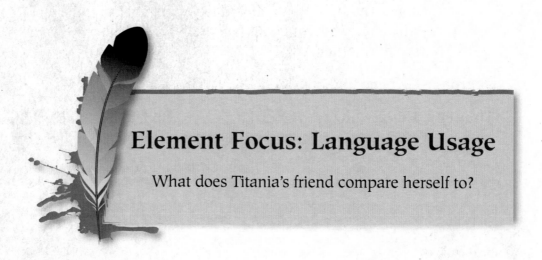

Element Focus: Language Usage

What does Titania's friend compare herself to?

A Midsummer Night's Dream

Act II, Scene I

Titania: Please calm down. This child that you want to take from me is not mine. Her mother was a good friend of mine. We used to sit together in the cool night air and talk. We loved to sit together on the beach to smell the salt air and watch the waves. We would watch as the ships came into the harbor with their treasures. She would compare herself to the ships' sails. They would grow round and fat when filled with the wind. She said it was just like her round and fat belly that held her baby. Often, she would go into the town and bring me back something special from the ships. But she was not a fairy like we are. No, she was human, and like all humans, she could die. When her baby was born into the world, she died and was taken away. But because she was such a wonderful friend, I promised to raise her child. And because I made such a promise, I will not allow you to have the child.

Oberon: How long are you planning to stay in these woods?

Titania: Maybe until after Theseus's wedding. If you will be kind and patient, come and be with us. If you will insist on behaving rudely, please leave. I will stay away from your favorite places so that we do not have to see each other.

Oberon: Give me that boy. Then I will happily stay with you.

Titania: There is no way you can have this child. Come, all my fairies, we must leave. Oberon and I will have a terrible fight if we stay here.

Exit Titania with her fairies

Oberon: That is fine, Titania. But be warned that I will punish you for not giving me what I want. My servant, Puck, come here. Do you remember the time we sat on that island? It was out in the ocean. Remember how we listened to that mermaid singing? And how she rode on the back of that dolphin?

Puck: I remember.

Oberon: While you were listening to her song, I saw something. Up in the sky, Cupid was flying. He had with him his bow and arrow. As you watched the mermaid, he shot an arrow down into a meadow on the island. I watched the arrow as it flew and saw where it landed. In the meadow, there was a white flower that young ladies liked to stop and smell. But when that flower was hit with Cupid's arrow, it turned purple. It was as if the flower had been bruised by the arrow. Go and get that flower for me. The juice of that flower has a special power. When it is put on the eyelids of someone sleeping, it will make the sleeper fall in love with the first live creature he or she sees after waking up. Hurry and go get that flower for me.

Puck: I will be there and back in no time at all.

Exit

Oberon: Once I have this flower, I will use it on Titania. I will put the juice of the flower on her eyes and make her fall in love with something horrible. Maybe a bear or an ape or a lion. And because she has the juice in her eyes, she will love the monster with her whole heart. Then I will be able to get that child from her. Wait, I hear someone coming. I will become invisible and hear what they have to say.

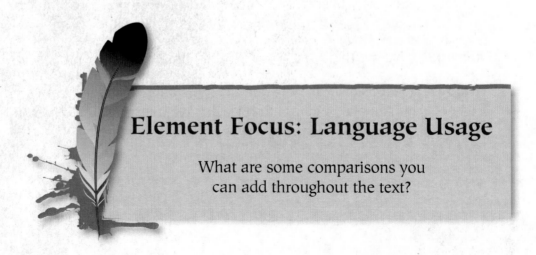

Element Focus: Language Usage

What are some comparisons you can add throughout the text?

#50982—*Leveled Texts for Classic Fiction: Shakespeare*

A Midsummer Night's Dream

Act II, Scene I

Titania: Please calm down, Oberon. This child that you want to take from me is not my child but the child of a good friend of mine. We used to sit together on the yellow sands of the beach in the cool night air and talk. We loved the smell of the salty air and the crisp sounds of the waves crashing on the shores. Together we would watch as the ships came into the harbor with their treasures, and she would compare her rounded belly with the ships' sails. She would laugh at how the sails became curved and full with the wind and say that they looked like her plump belly that held her baby. Often, she would go into the town, her huge belly draped with flowing sheets of clothes, and bring me back special treats from the ships. But she was not a fairy like we are, Oberon. No, she was human, and like all humans, she could die. When her baby was born into the world, she died and was taken away from me. But when she died, I vowed that I would raise her child, and because I made such a promise to her, I will not allow you to have the child.

Oberon: How long are you planning to stay in these woods?

Titania: Maybe until after Theseus's wedding. If you will be kind and patient, come and be with us to help celebrate the wedding. But if you will insist on behaving rudely and demanding that I hand over the boy, I will ask you to please leave. While we are in these woods together, I will stay away from your favorite places so that we do not have to see each other.

Oberon: Give me that boy, and I will happily stay with you for as long as you wish.

Titania: There is no way you can have this child. Come, all my fairies, we must leave. Oberon and I will have a terrible fight if we stay here any longer.

Exit Titania with her fairies

Oberon: That is fine that you leave, Titania, but be warned that I will punish you for not giving me what I want. My servant, Puck, come here. Do you remember the time we sat on that island out in the ocean? Remember how we listened to that beautiful mermaid singing a song and how she rode on the back of that dolphin?

Puck: I remember.

Oberon: While you were listening to her song, I saw something that you did not see. Up in the sky, Cupid was flying with his bow and arrow. As you watched the mermaid, he shot an arrow down into a meadow on the island, and I watched as the arrow flew and as it landed. In the meadow, there was a white flower that young ladies liked to stop and smell. But when that white flower was hit with Cupid's arrow, it turned purple, as if it had been bruised by the arrow. Go and get that flower for me. It is important because the juice of that flower has a special power. When it is put on the eyelids of someone sleeping, it will make the sleeper fall madly in love with the first live creature he or she sees upon waking. Hurry and go get that flower for me.

Puck: I will be there and back in no time at all.

Exit

Oberon: Once I have this flower, I will use it against Titania. I will put the juice of it on her eyes and make her fall in love with something horrible, like a bear or an ape or a lion. Because she has the juice in her eyes, she will love this monster with her whole heart and be so distracted that I will be able to get that child from her. Wait, I hear someone coming. I will become invisible and hear what they have to say.

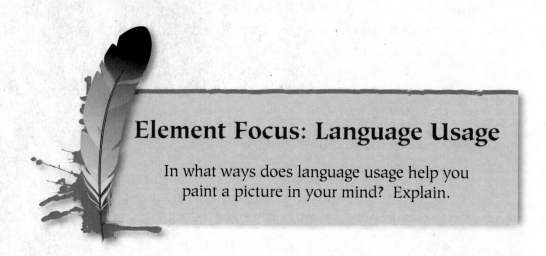

Element Focus: Language Usage

In what ways does language usage help you paint a picture in your mind? Explain.

Excerpt from

A Midsummer Night's Dream

Act II, Scene I

Titania: This child that you wish to take from me is not my own but belongs to a wonderful friend of mine. During her pregnancy, we used to sit together on the yellow sands of the beach on cool evenings, smelling the salty air. Together we would watch as the ships came into the harbor; heavy with their treasures, and she would compare her rounded pregnant belly with the ships' full sails. Laughing, she would talk about how the sails would billow out  curved and full with the wind and say that they resembled her own plump and fleshy belly that held her baby. Often, she would go into the town, her huge belly draped with flowing sheets of clothes, and bring me back special treats. But she was not an immortal fairy like we are. No, she was human, and like all humans, she could die. When her baby was born into the world, she died and was taken away from me; but as she died, I vowed that I would raise her child. For her sake, I have pledged to nurture this child, and I will not allow you to have the child.

Oberon: How long are you planning to stay in these woods?

Titania: Maybe until after Theseus's wedding. If you will be kind and patient, you can come along with us to celebrate the wedding; but if you will insist on behaving rudely and demanding that I hand over the boy, I will ask you to please leave. While we are in these woods together, I will stay away from your favorite places so that we do not have to see each other and run the risk of beginning another fight.

Oberon: Give me that boy, and I will happily stay with you for as long as you wish.

Titania: There is no way you can have this child. Come, all my fairies, we must leave now, because Oberon and I will have a terrible fight if we stay here any longer.

Exit Titania with her fairies

Oberon: That is fine that you leave, Titania, but be warned that I will punish and humiliate you for not giving me what I want. My servant, Puck, come here. Do you remember the time we sat on that island out in the ocean, listening to that beautiful mermaid singing a song, and how she rode on the back of that dolphin?

Puck: I remember.

Oberon: While you were listening to her song, I saw something that you did not see. Up in the sky, Cupid was flying with his bow and arrow. As you watched the mermaid, I saw him shoot an arrow down into a meadow on the island, and I watched as the arrow flew and as it landed. In the meadow where Cupid shot, there was a white flower, but when that white flower was hit with Cupid's arrow, it turned purple, as if it had been bruised. Go and get that flower for me. It is important because the juice of that flower has a special power. When it is put on the eyelids of someone sleeping, it will make the sleeper fall madly in love with the first live creature he or she sees upon waking. Hurry, Puck, and go get that flower for me.

Puck: I will be there and back in no time at all.

Exit

Oberon: Once I have this flower, I will use it against Titania. I will put the juice of it on her eyes and make her fall in love with something horrible, like a bear or an ape or a lion. Because she has the juice in her eyes, she will love this monster with her whole heart and be so distracted that I will be able to get that child from her. Wait, I hear someone coming. I will become invisible and hear what they have to say.

Element Focus: Language Usage

Circle words from Titania's speech that show how she feels about the child's mother. Circle words spoken by Oberon that show how he wants Titania to feel. Why does the author use this type of language?

Excerpt from

Romeo and Juliet

Act II, Scene II

Romeo: But wait! There is a beautiful light in that window. What is it? Oh, it is the pretty Juliet. She is so lovely that she is like the sun. Everything around her looks pale and sick because she is so bright. Juliet is my lady and my love. I wish that she knew how much I loved her and that I did not have to hide here under her window. I love every part of her. Wait, she is speaking. But sadly, it is not to me. Her eyes are stars. The night sky is missing two glowing and beautiful stars because they are shining brightly in Juliet's face. Her face is so pretty and light that she almost turns the night into day. I think I can hear the birds singing. They see the light of Juliet's eyes and believe she is the sun. And look how she puts that beautiful face in her hands. I wish that I could be those hands, and touch that lovely face. That I might touch that cheek!

Juliet: Oh my!

Romeo: Juliet talks. Talk to me, lovely Juliet. You are the most wonderful thing I have ever seen. You look like a glowing white angel.

Juliet: Romeo. Romeo! Why are you named Romeo? Can you give up your name? I will be yours if you will. But if you cannot give up your name, I will give up mine. Tell me you love me, and I will stop being Juliet Capulet.

Romeo: [Aside] Should I stay and hear what she has to say? Or should I speak to her now?

Juliet: It is not you my family dislikes. It is your name they dislike, but you are not just your name. There is more to you than just a name. You are made up of many parts. Which one of those parts is only your name? How important is a name? A rose smells sweet under any name. It does not matter if I call it a rose because it will still smell the same. You are like that rose. You are my love, and you would still be my love even if I called you something else. Throw away your name, Romeo. And then I can give you all of my love.

Romeo: Then I will never be called Romeo again.

Juliet: Who is there? It is a dark night, and I cannot see who is out there.

Romeo: How can I tell you my name? You just told me that I should throw my name away. I would give it away for your love. If I had my name written on a paper, I would tear it into pieces.

Juliet: I know that voice. I have not heard much of your voice. But I know it. Is that Romeo who speaks?

Romeo: I will be whomever you want. If you do not want me to be Romeo, I will be someone else.

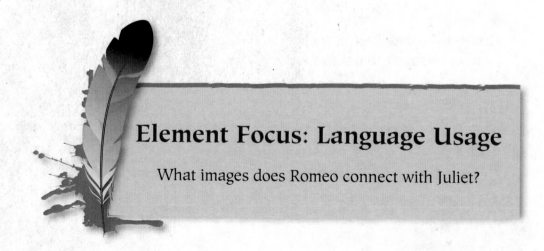

Element Focus: Language Usage

What images does Romeo connect with Juliet?

Excerpt from

Romeo and Juliet

Act II, Scene II

Romeo: But wait, there is a beautiful light in that window. Oh, it is the lovely Juliet. She is so beautiful that she shines with the brightness of the sun. Her own light is so strong that it makes everything around her look pale and sick. From this moment on, Juliet is my lady and my love. I wish that I could speak to her and let her understand how much I love her. Instead, I have to hide here under her window. I love every part of her. If her eyes were the only things that would look at me, I would be happy with just having her eyes love me. Wait, she is speaking, but sadly it is not to me. Her eyes are shining stars lighting the dark night. The night sky is missing two glowing and brilliant stars because they are shining brightly in Juliet's face. Her face is so pretty and light that she almost turns the night into day. I think I can hear the birds singing even though it is night. They see the light of Juliet's eyes and believe she is the sun. And look how she puts that beautiful face in her hands. I wish that I could be those hands and touch that lovely face.

Juliet: Oh my!

Romeo: Juliet speaks. Talk to me, lovely Juliet. You are the most wonderful thing I have ever seen. You are a white angel who has come from the heavens to bring me your love and your light.

Juliet: Romeo. Romeo! Why are you named Romeo? Can you give up your name, Romeo? If you would be willing to throw away your name, I would be yours forever. But if you cannot give up your name, I will give up mine. Tell me you love me, and I will stop being Juliet Capulet.

Romeo: [Aside] Should I stay and hear what she has to say? Or should I have the courage to speak to her now?

Juliet: Romeo, it is not you my family dislikes. It is your name they dislike, Romeo Montague. But you are so much more than just a name. You are made up of so many parts, like arms and legs and hands. Which one of those single parts is only your name? How important is a name? When I smell a rose, it smells sweet and it does not matter if I call that flower a rose or if I call it something else. No matter what I call that flower, it will always smell sweet. Romeo, you are like that rose. You are my love, and you would still be my love even if I called you something else. Throw away your name, Romeo, and when you are no longer called Romeo, I can give you all of my love.

Romeo: Then I will never be called Romeo again.

Juliet: Who is there in the night? There is only darkness around me, and I cannot see who is speaking to me.

Romeo: How can I tell you my name? You just told me that I should throw my name away, and to earn your love, I would do it. If I had my name written on a paper, I would tear it into pieces.

Juliet: I know that voice, even though I have not heard it much. Is that Romeo who speaks?

Romeo: I will be whomever you want me to be, Juliet. If you do not want me to be Romeo, I will be someone else.

Element Focus: Language Usage

Romeo connects Juliet to light. Why does the author make this connection?

Excerpt from

Romeo and Juliet

Act II, Scene II

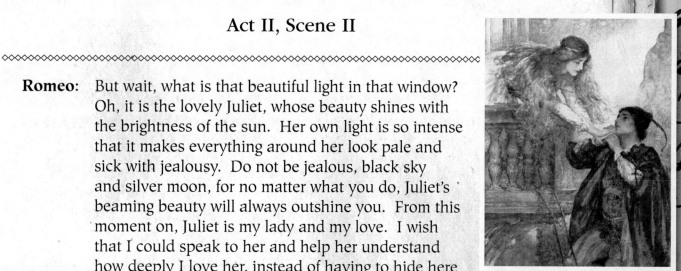

Romeo: But wait, what is that beautiful light in that window? Oh, it is the lovely Juliet, whose beauty shines with the brightness of the sun. Her own light is so intense that it makes everything around her look pale and sick with jealousy. Do not be jealous, black sky and silver moon, for no matter what you do, Juliet's beaming beauty will always outshine you. From this moment on, Juliet is my lady and my love. I wish that I could speak to her and help her understand how deeply I love her, instead of having to hide here in the shadows beneath her window. I love every individual and tiny part of her. If her eyes were the only things that would notice me, I would be filled with joy that her eyes would look at me. Wait, she is speaking, but sadly it is not to me. Her eyes are perfect, glowing stars lighting the dark night. The night sky is missing two shimmering and brilliant stars because they are shining brightly in Juliet's face. Her face is so glorious and light that she almost turns the darkness of the night into the clear light of day. I think I can hear the birds singing in confusion. They see the light of Juliet's eyes and, believing she is the sun, they awake to sing their morning song. And look how she rests that breathtaking face in her soft hands. I long to be a glove on those hands, and I long to be allowed to touch that lovely face.

Juliet: Oh my!

Romeo: Juliet speaks; speak to me, lovely Juliet. You are the most magnificent thing I have ever seen, a white angel who has come from the heavens to bring me love and light.

Juliet: Romeo, oh Romeo! Why are you named Romeo? Can you break away from your name, Romeo? If you would be willing to release yourself from your name, I would be yours forever. But if it is impossible to leave your name, Romeo, I will give up mine. Tell me you love me, and I will never again be called Juliet Capulet.

Romeo: [Aside] Should I stay and hear what she has to say, or should I have the courage to speak to her now as she confesses her love for me?

Juliet: Romeo, it is not you that my family despises, but it is your name that is my enemy. Your name: Romeo Montague. But how can that be when you are so much more than just a name? Romeo is made up of so many little parts, like hands and arms and legs, but which one of those individual parts is your name? How can your name be the only thing that determines who you are? When I smell a rose, it smells sweet regardless of the name that I give it. It does not matter if I call that flower a rose or if I call it something else. Romeo, you are like that rose because even if I call you something other than Romeo, you will still be the young man who has my love and my heart. Throw away your name, Romeo, and when you are no longer called Romeo, I can give you all of my love.

Romeo: Then I will never be called Romeo again.

Juliet: Who is there in the night? There is only darkness around me, and I cannot see who is speaking to me.

Romeo: How can I tell you my name, sweet Juliet, when you have just told me that I should throw my name away? If my name is hateful to you, then it is hateful to me. If I had my name written on a paper, I would tear it into pieces.

Juliet: I have heard your voice less than one hundred times, but I already feel as if I know it. Is that Romeo who speaks?

Romeo: I will be whomever you want me to be, Juliet. If you do not want me to be Romeo, I will be someone else.

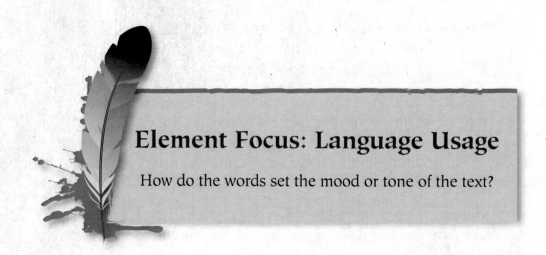

Element Focus: Language Usage

How do the words set the mood or tone of the text?

Excerpt from

Romeo and Juliet

Act II, Scene II

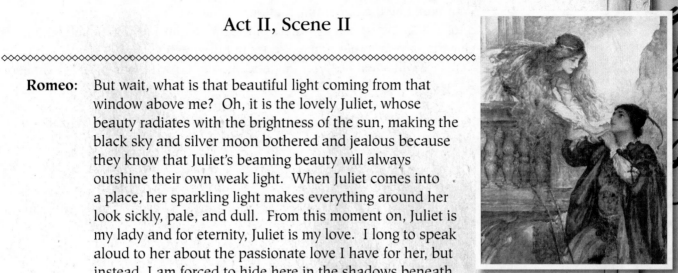

Romeo: But wait, what is that beautiful light coming from that window above me? Oh, it is the lovely Juliet, whose beauty radiates with the brightness of the sun, making the black sky and silver moon bothered and jealous because they know that Juliet's beaming beauty will always outshine their own weak light. When Juliet comes into a place, her sparkling light makes everything around her look sickly, pale, and dull. From this moment on, Juliet is my lady and for eternity, Juliet is my love. I long to speak aloud to her about the passionate love I have for her, but instead, I am forced to hide here in the shadows beneath her window. I love every single and individual part of her and would find happiness in any part Juliet would be willing to bestow on me. If her eyes were the only things that would notice me, I would be filled with joy for the simple fact that her eyes would look at me. Wait, she is speaking, but unfortunately, she is not speaking to me. Her eyes are perfect, glowing stars lighting the dark night, and the sky weeps with sorrow for the two missing stars that have left the gloom of night to shimmer brilliantly in Juliet's face. It is a face so glorious and light that it almost turns the murky dark of the night into the clear and visible light of day. I think I can hear the birds that see the light of Juliet's eyes and, believing she is the sun, they awake to sing their morning song in confusion. And look how she gently rests that breathtaking face in her soft hands. I long to be a glove on those hands, and I long to be allowed to caress that lovely face.

Juliet: Oh my!

Romeo: Juliet speaks; speak to me, lovely Juliet. You are the most magnificent thing I have ever seen, a white angel who has floated from the heavens to bring light and love to my sorry life.

Juliet: Romeo, oh Romeo! Why are you named Romeo? Can you break away from your name, Romeo? If you will release yourself from your name, I would be yours forever, but if it is impossible for you to leave your name, Romeo, I will give up mine. Tell me you love me, and I will never again be called Juliet Capulet.

Romeo: [Aside] Should I stay and hear what she has to say, or should I have the courage to speak to her now as she confesses her love for me?

Juliet: Romeo, it is not you that my family despises, but it is your name that is my enemy. Your name alone is the barrier between our love: Romeo Montague. But how can a name inspire hatred when you are so much more than just a name? Romeo is made up of so many different parts, like hands and arms and legs, but which one of those individual parts is your name? How can your name be the only thing that determines who you are? When I smell a rose, it smells sweet regardless of the name that I give it. If suddenly I give that rose another name, it does not diminish the sweet smell. Oh no, that rose will smell of sweet fragrance no matter what name I place on it. Romeo, you are like that rose because even if I call you something other than Romeo, you will still be the young man who has my love and my heart. Throw away your name, Romeo, and when you are no longer called Romeo, I can give you all of my love.

Romeo: Then I will never be called Romeo again.

Juliet: Who is there in the night? There is only darkness around me, and I cannot see who is speaking to me.

Romeo: How can I tell you my name, sweet Juliet, when you have just told me that I would earn your eternal love if I would throw my name away? If my name is hateful to you, then it is hateful to me. If I had my name written on a paper, I would tear it into pieces.

Juliet: I have heard your voice less than one hundred times, but I already feel as if I know it. Is that Romeo who speaks?

Romeo: I will be whomever you want me to be, Juliet. If you do not want me to be Romeo, I will be someone else.

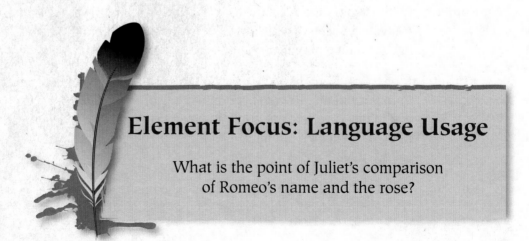

Element Focus: Language Usage

What is the point of Juliet's comparison of Romeo's name and the rose?

#50982—Leveled Texts for Classic Fiction: Shakespeare

Excerpt from

The Taming of the Shrew

Act II, Scene I

Petruchio: I will wait here for her to come. When she does come to see me, I will speak loving words to her even if she acts with anger. Maybe she will scream and yell. If she does, I will tell her that her voice is beautiful like the voice of a bird. Maybe she will frown and make ugly faces at me. If she does, I will tell her that she is the most beautiful woman I have ever seen. Maybe she will not speak and will choose not to talk with me at all. If she does, I will tell her that she speaks with pretty words and amazes me with her brain. Maybe she will tell me to leave at once. If she does, I will thank her for being so kind and generous. Maybe she will say that she will never marry me. If she does, I will tell her I cannot wait to be her husband. Then, I will ask her father when we can have the wedding. Oh wait. Here she comes.

Enter Katharina

Good day, Kate. May I call you Kate? I hear that is your name.

Katharina: If you have heard that, you were not listening very well. People who talk about me call me Katharina.

Petruchio: Oh no, no, Kate. You are called so many things, Kate. You are called lovely Kate. Sometimes they call you beautiful Kate or Kate who is cursed with grace. But to me, you are the prettiest Kate I have ever seen. And so, Kate, who is all my heart, I want to tell you something. I have traveled all over the land. During my travels, I have heard so much about you. How you are a sweet, slow to anger, and honorable woman. And after hearing all of this praise, my heart told me to move toward you. And I want to ask your heart to be moved near to me, and to be my wife.

Katharina: You want my heart to move! The only thing moving is going to be you. Now take yourself away. You can choose how you move. Just make sure that you move away from me.

Petruchio: But I will be your husband. I will not be moved away. What kind of man is sent away without a fight for you?

Katharina: Most men are dumber than a chair.

Petruchio: Oh, if you want a place to rest, then come and sit on my lap.

Katharina: You may put your rear anywhere you want. But leave mine alone.

Petruchio: All of you will belong to me when you are my wife.

Katharina: You are crazy if you think I will be your wife.

Petruchio: Oh Kate. Stop acting this way. I know you are young. Your beauty is a light that shines on me.

Katharina: Yes, I am light. Light enough that I can simply fly away. A big heavy man like you can never catch me.

Petruchio: Do not fly away like a bird.

Katharina: No, I fly more like a bee.

Petruchio: No, no, Kate. Not a bee. They are too angry.

Katharina: Yes, and any man better be careful because like a bee, I have a powerful stinger.

Petruchio: I know how to get around a stinger. I will pull it out.

Katharina: But you can only pull it out if you can find it.

Petruchio: Everyone knows a bee's stinger is in his tail.

Katharina: No, mine is in my tongue. I can sting with my sharp words.

Petruchio: Not your tongue, Kate. Not my wonderful Kate.

Katharina: You may say whatever words you want, but I will not listen.

Petruchio: Yes, you will Kate. You will make your pointed tongue less sharp, and we will be married.

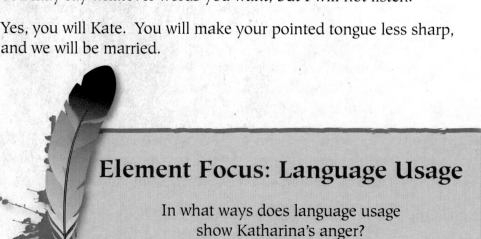

Element Focus: Language Usage

In what ways does language usage
show Katharina's anger?

#50982—*Leveled Texts for Classic Fiction: Shakespeare* © *Shell Education*

The Taming of the Shrew

Act II, Scene I

Petruchio: I will wait here for her to come. When she does come to see me, I will speak loving words to her even if she acts with anger. Maybe she will scream and yell, but if she does, I will tell her that her voice is beautiful like the voice of a bird. Maybe she will frown and make ugly faces at me, but if she does, I will tell her that she is the most beautiful woman I have ever seen. Maybe she will not speak and will choose not to talk with me at all, but if she does, I will tell her that she speaks with pretty words and amazes me with her brain. Maybe she will tell me to leave at once, but if she does, I will thank her for being so kind and generous. Maybe she will say that she will never marry me, but if she does, I will tell her I cannot wait to be her husband. Then, I will ask her father when we can have the wedding. Oh wait, here she comes.

Enter Katharina

Good day, Kate. May I call you Kate? I hear that is your name.

Katharina: If you have heard that, you were not listening very well, because people who talk about me call me Katharina.

Petruchio: Oh no, no Kate, you are called so many things, Kate. You are called lovely Kate, or sometimes they call you beautiful Kate, maybe even Kate who is cursed with grace. But to me, you are the prettiest Kate I have ever seen; and so, Kate, who is all my heart, I want to tell you something. I have traveled throughout the land and have heard so much about you. I have heard stories of how you are a sweet, patient, and honorable woman. And after hearing all of this praise, my heart told me to move toward you. So I have come here to ask your heart to be moved near to me and to be my wife.

Katharina: You want my heart to move! The only thing moving is going to be you when you take yourself away. You can choose how and when and where you move—just make sure that you move away from me.

Petruchio: But I will be your husband, and I will not be moved away. What kind of man is sent away without a fight for you?

Katharina: Most men are dumber than a chair.

Petruchio: Oh, if you want a place to rest, then come and sit on my lap.

Katharina: You may put your rear anywhere you want, but leave mine alone.

Petruchio: All of you will belong to me when you are my wife.

Katharina: You are crazy if you think I will be your wife.

Petruchio: Oh Kate, stop acting this way. I know you are young, but your beauty is a light that shines on me.

Katharina: Yes, I am light. Light enough that I can simply fly away, and a big heavy man like you can never catch me.

Petruchio: Do not fly away like a bird.

Katharina: No, I fly more like a bee.

Petruchio: No, no, Kate, not a bee. They are too angry.

Katharina: Yes, and any man should be careful because like a bee, I have a powerful stinger.

Petruchio: I know how to get around a stinger. I will pull it out.

Katharina: But you can only pull it out if you can find it.

Petruchio: Everyone knows a bee's stinger is in his tail.

Katharina: No, mine is in my tongue because I sting with my sharp words.

Petruchio: Not your tongue, Kate. Not my wonderful Kate.

Katharina: You may say whatever words you want, but I will not listen.

Petruchio: Yes, you will, Kate. You will make your pointed tongue less sharp, and we will be married.

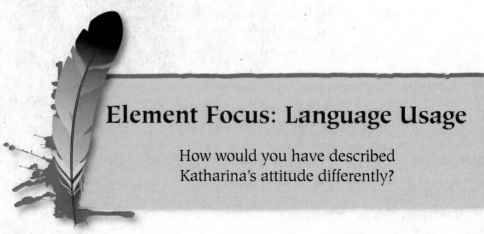

Element Focus: Language Usage

How would you have described Katharina's attitude differently?

#50982—Leveled Texts for Classic Fiction: Shakespeare

Excerpt from

The Taming of the Shrew

Act II, Scene I

◇◇◇

Petruchio: I will wait here for her to come, and when she does, I will speak adoring words to her even if she speaks with cruel words inspired by her temper. Perhaps she will scream and throw words of rage at me, but if she does, I will tell her that her voice is like the voice of a bird. Perhaps she will frown, turning her face into ugly shapes, but if she does, I will tell her that she is the most beautiful woman I have ever seen. Perhaps she will refuse to speak and stubbornly ignore me, but if she does, I will tell her that she speaks with such intelligence and creativity that she amazes me with her brain. Perhaps she will demand that I leave at once, but if she does, I will thank her for being so kind and hospitable. Perhaps she will say that she will never marry me, but I will tell her I am impatient to be her husband and will ask her father. Then, when we can have the wedding. Oh wait, here she comes.

Enter Katharina

Good day, Kate. May I call you Kate, for I hear that is your name?

Katharina: If you have heard that, you were clearly not listening very well, because people who dare to talk about me call me Katharina.

Petruchio: Oh no, no Kate, you are wrong, for you are called so many things, Kate. You are called lovely Kate, or sometimes they call you beautiful Kate, maybe even Kate who is cursed with grace; but to me you are the prettiest Kate I have ever seen. And so, I want to tell you that I have traveled throughout the land and have heard so much about you. I have heard stories of how you are a sweet, easygoing, and honorable woman. And after hearing all of this praise, my heart told me to move toward you. So I have come here to ask your heart to be moved near to me and to be my wife.

Katharina: You want my heart to move! The only thing moving between the two of us is going to be you when you take yourself away. You can choose how and when—just make sure that you move away from me.

Petruchio: But I will be your husband, and I will not be moved away. What kind of man is sent away without a fight for you?

Katharina: Most men are dumber than a chair.

Petruchio: Oh, if you want a place to rest, then come and sit on my lap.

Katharina: You may put your rear anywhere you want, but leave mine alone.

Petruchio: All of you will belong to me when you are my wife.

Katharina: You are crazy if you think any part of me will be your wife.

Petruchio: Oh Kate, stop acting this way. I know you are young, but your beauty is a light that shines on me.

Katharina: Yes, I am light. So light, in fact, that I can simply fly away, and a big heavy man like you can never catch me.

Petruchio: Do not fly away like a bird.

Katharina: No, I am not a bird. I fly more like a bee.

Petruchio: No, no, Kate, you are not a bee. They are too angry.

Katharina: Buzz, buzz, and any man should be careful because like a bee, I have a powerful and painful stinger.

Petruchio: I can get around a stinger, Kate, because all I have to do is pull it out.

Katharina: But you can only pull it out if you are smart enough to find it.

Petruchio: Even a fool knows a bee's stinger is in his tail.

Katharina: Then you are a fool, for mine is not hidden in so obvious a place. No, mine is in my tongue because I sting and wound with my sharp words.

Petruchio: Not your tongue, Kate. Not my wonderful Kate.

Katharina: You may say whatever words you want, but believe me, I will not listen.

Petruchio: Yes, you will Kate. You will use your tongue to sing soft expressions of love and not to pierce me, and that will begin when we are married.

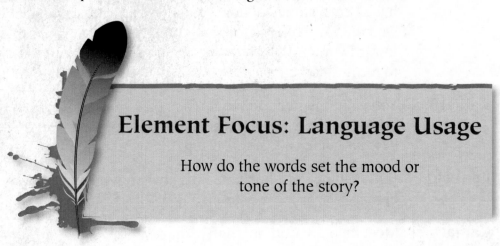

Element Focus: Language Usage

How do the words set the mood or
tone of the story?

Excerpt from

The Taming of the Shrew

Act II, Scene I

Petruchio: I will wait calmly here for her to come, and when she does, I will speak adoringly and affectionately to her even if she responds in a passionate fit with cruel words inspired by her temper. Perhaps when we meet, she will scream hysterically, but I will say that her voice is as pleasing as the voice of a bird. Perhaps she will frown, turning her face into ugly shapes, but I will say that she is the most beautiful woman I have ever seen. Perhaps she will refuse to speak, stubbornly ignore me, and pretend that I am not present, but if she does, I will say that she astounds me. Perhaps she will insist that I leave at once, but if she does, I will thank her for being so generous, so welcoming, and so hospitable. Perhaps she will say that she will never marry me, but if she does, I will say I am impatient to be her husband and will ask her father if we can hold the wedding soon. Oh wait, here she comes.

Enter Katharina

Good day, Kate. May I have permission to call you Kate, since I hear that is your name?

Katharina: If you have heard that, you were clearly not listening very well, because people who dare to talk about me call me Katharina.

Petruchio: Oh no, no Kate, you are wrong, for you are called so many things, Kate. Throughout this city, you are called lovely Kate, or sometimes they call you beautiful Kate, maybe even Kate who is cursed with grace; but to me, you are the prettiest Kate I have ever seen. And so, Kate, who is all my heart, Kate who is all my world, I want to tell you that I have traveled throughout the land and having heard stories of how you are a sweet, easygoing, quiet woman who never uses words to make others feel insignificant, my heart told me to come and to ask your heart to be moved near to me and to be my wife.

Katharina: You want my heart to move! The only thing moving between the two of us is going to be you. You can choose how and when and where you move yourself—just make sure that you move away from me.

Petruchio: But I am determined to be your husband, and I will not be moved away. What kind of man is sent away without a fight for you?

Katharina: Sadly, most men are not aware that they are dumber than a chair.

Petruchio: Oh, if you want a place to relax, then come sit on my lap.

Katharina: You may put your rear anywhere you desire, but leave mine alone.

Petruchio: All of you will belong to me when you are my wife.

Katharina: You are crazy if you think any part of me will be your wife.

Petruchio: Oh Kate, stop acting this way. I know you are young, but your beauty is a light that shines on me.

Katharina: Yes, I am light. So light, in fact, that I can simply fly away, and a big heavy man like you can never catch me.

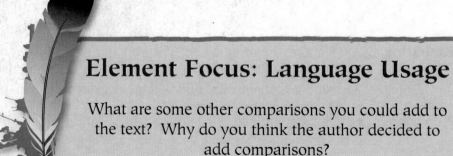

Petruchio: Do not fly away like a bird.

Katharina: No, I am not a bird. I fly more like a bee.

Petruchio: No, no, Kate, you are not a bee. They are too angry.

Katharina: Buzz, buzz, and any man should be careful because like a bee, I have a powerful and painful stinger.

Petruchio: I can get around a stinger, even yours, because all I have to do is pull it out.

Katharina: But you can only pull it out if you are clever enough to find it.

Petruchio: Even a fool knows a bee's stinger is in his tail.

Katharina: No, mine is in my tongue because I sting and wound with my words.

Petruchio: Not your tongue, Kate. Not my wonderful Kate.

Katharina: You may say whatever decorated words you think might impress me, but believe me when I say I will not listen.

Petruchio: Yes, you will, Kate. You will use your tongue to sing soft expressions of love rather than pierce me with harsh words, and that will begin when we are married.

Element Focus: Language Usage

What are some other comparisons you could add to the text? Why do you think the author decided to add comparisons?

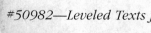

References Cited

Bean, Thomas. 2000. Reading in the Content Areas: Social Constructivist Dimensions. In *Handbook of Reading Research, vol. 3*, eds. M. Kamil, P. Mosenthal, P. D. Pearson, and R. Barr. Mahwah, NJ: Lawrence Erlbaum.

Bromley, Karen. 2004. Rethinking Vocabulary Instruction. *The Language and Literacy Spectrum* 14:3–12.

Melville, Herman. 1851. *Moby Dick*. New York: Harper.

Nagy, William, and Richard C. Anderson. 1984. How Many Words Are There in Printed School English? *Reading Research Quarterly* 19 (3): 304–330.

National Governors Association Center for Best Practices and Council of Chief State School Officers. 2010. Common Core Standards. http://www.corestandards.org/the-standards.

Oatley, Keith. 2009. Changing Our Minds. *Greater Good: The Science of a Meaningful Life*, Winter. http://greatergood.berkeley.edu/article/item/chaning_our_minds.

Pinnell, Gay Su. 1988. Success of Children At Risk in a Program that Combines Writing and Reading. *Technical Report No.* 417 (January). Reading and Writing Connections.

Richek, Margaret. 2005. Words Are Wonderful: Interactive, Time-Efficient Strategies to Teach Meaning Vocabulary. *The Reading Teacher* 58 (5): 414–423.

Riordan, Rick. 2005. *The Lightning Thief*. London: Puffin Books.

Sachar, Louis. 2000. *Holes*. New York, NY: Dell Yearling.

Snicket, Lemony. 1999. *A Series of Unfortunate Events*. New York: HarperCollins.

Tomlinson, Carol Ann and Marcia. B. Imbeau. 2010. *Leading and Managing a Differentiated Classroom*. Alexandria, VA: Association for Supervision and Curriculum Development.

Zunshine, Lisa. 2006. *Why We Read Fiction: Theory of Mind and the Novel*. Columbus, OH: The Ohio State University Press.

Contents of the Digital Resource CD

Passage	Filename	Pages
Twelfth Night—Act I, Scene II	twelfth.pdf twelfth.doc originaltwelfth.pdf	31–38
Julius Caesar—Act I, Scene I	juliuscaesar.pdf juliuscaesar.doc originaljulius.pdf	39–46
The Tempest—Act I, Scene I	tempest.pdf tempest.doc originaltempest.pdf	47–54
Henry V—Act VI, Scene III	henryv.pdf henryv.doc originalhenryv.pdf	55–62
Othello—Act I, Scene III	othello.pdf othello.doc originalothello.pdf	63–70
Richard III—Act I, Scene I	richard.pdf richard.doc originalrichard.pdf	71–78
The Winter's Tale—Act II, Scene II	winterstale.pdf winterstale.doc originalwinterstale.pdf	79–86
Hamlet—Act IV, Scene VII	hamlet.pdf hamlet.doc originalhamlet.pdf	87–94
King Lear—Act I, Scene I	kinglear.pdf kinglear.doc originalkinglear.pdf	95–102
Macbeth—Act I, Scene VII	macbeth.pdf macbeth.doc originalmacbeth.pdf	103–110
Much Ado About Nothing—Act II, Scene III	muchado.pdf muchado.doc originalmuchado.pdf	111–118
The Merchant of Venice—Act V, Scene I	merchant.pdf merchant.doc originalmerchant.pdf	119–126
A Midsummer Night's Dream—Act II, Scene I	midsummer.pdf midsummer.doc originalmidsummer.pdf	127–134
Romeo and Juliet—Act II, Scene II	romeojuliet.pdf romeojuliet.doc originalromeo.pdf	135–142
The Taming of the Shrew—Act II, Scene I	tamingshrew.pdf tamingshrew.doc originaltaming.pdf	143–150